the
best-laid
plans

OTHER BOOKS AND AUDIOBOOKS
BY SARAH M. EDEN

CHRONOLOGICAL ORDER OF ALL RELATED
SARAH M. EDEN GEORGIAN- & REGENCY-ERA BOOKS

SARAH M. EDEN

the best-laid plans

A HUNTRESSES REGENCY ROMANCE

Covenant Communications, Inc.

Cover image © Laura Kate Ranftler / Arcangel
Cover design by Michelle Fryer

Cover design copyright © 2021 by Covenant Communications, Inc.

Published by Covenant Communications, Inc.
American Fork, Utah

Printed in Mexico
First Printing: August 2022

28 27 26 25 24 23 22   10 9 8 7 6 5 4 3 2 1

ISBN 978-1-52442-209-7

CHAPTER ONE

Bath, 1817

NEWTON HUGHES WAS A GENTLEMAN, which was a shame, really. Gentlemen's options were limited.

"You are not in need of a profession." Father lowered the book he was reading. His mouth twisted, and his brow creased heavily. "To take one up unnecessarily undermines your standing. Our family's standing."

Newton and his parents had been passing a peaceful evening in the drawing room of the family's Bath home when Newton had made the mistake of mentioning his ambitions. His long-standing interest in the law was not motivated by low standing that would be improved by the profession.

"I do not discount nor disregard our family's social cachet." He crossed to the nearby mantelpiece, hoping that by anchoring himself, he could resist the urge to pace. "Few hostesses are as rightly praised as Mother." He dipped his head to her, sitting beside Father on the sofa.

Mother smiled at him over her needlepoint. "Now that your time at Cambridge is over you simply must join Society. You've deprived them of your company long enough."

"I doubt they have been devastated by my absence."

"*I* have been," Mother said.

He suspected she hadn't been truly miserable without him nearby, but he appreciated the sentiment. "When the Season begins again next year, I vow to dance with you at each and every London ball I possibly can."

Father spoke once more. "You will not have time for dancing if you follow this foolhardy notion of attaching yourself to an Inn of Court—assuming, of course, Society invites you to any."

"A gentleman can be a barrister." Newton had reminded his parents of that again and again.

"Gentlemen *from struggling families* can be barristers." Father motioned broadly to the silk-hung walls, marble fireplace, and elegant furnishings that adorned this lesser home amongst the family's many holdings. "I am an able and responsible steward of my estate. The income you receive from it is more than sufficient."

"The Earl of Lampton has a brother who is a barrister," Newton reminded him. "One cannot describe his family as struggling."

Father had no response to that, it seemed. Newton didn't for a moment think he'd actually convinced his father of anything. Sometimes he wondered if either of his parents understood him at all.

Mother set aside her sewing, quickly smoothed the front of her silk gown, and crossed to where Newton stood. She always looked elegant, even when spending a quiet night at home. She slipped her arm through Newton's and walked with him toward the other side of the drawing room. "You remain friends with the youngest of Lord Lampton's brothers, do you not?"

"I do, indeed." Newton's natural disposition would have seen him alone and isolated during his school years, but Charlie Jonquil had pulled him out into the world without trying to force him to be someone he wasn't. He was the best sort of friend.

"He is currently on term break, I believe."

Newton nodded, utterly unsure what Mother had in mind.

"How likely is he, do you think, to accept an invitation to join us in London for the Season?"

Charlie seldom went to London. Even if extending an invitation could convince him to jaunt up to Town, the timing was poor.

"He has not completed his studies at Cambridge," Newton said. "When the Season begins, he will be in the midst of Lent term."

Mother nodded. "I forget at times that he is a year younger than you are."

"And pursuing an academic field of endeavor," Newton added. "He has a great deal more schooling yet."

Mother stopped beneath one of the tall, diamond-paned windows and lowered her voice to a quiet whisper. "Your father is a little in awe of that family. He might spend less time criticizing you if a Jonquil is nearby."

"Charlie would act as my champion?" The idea was laughable. Charlie was far more likely to jest than to joust.

"I was thinking more of a shield, and one you would enjoy having nearby." She sighed a little. "I had hoped if you could have some assurance that your father would not torture you with this belabored topic, you might actually participate in the social whirl." She sounded a little too sad and a little too disappointed for his peace of mind.

"If only London were in the midst of that whirl now," Newton said. "Charlie is on term break for the next month."

Excitement lit her expression. "We will be in Bath for longer than that."

"I might be able to convince him to join us here."

Mother clapped her hands together, her eyes opening wide with anticipation. "Oh, Newton. He would force you into Society, I am certain of it."

"*Who* would force him?" Father had, apparently, overheard part of her last remark.

"Young Mr. Charles Jonquil." Mother turned to face the sofa, where he still sat.

"Jonquil? Excellent." He set his neglected book on the table beside him. He rose with a look of determination on his face. "I will begin seeing to the arrangements for travel forthwith."

"Let us hope Charlie agrees," Newton muttered.

Father crossed toward the door but turned back before leaving the room and looked directly at him. "Bath is perfect. No Inns of Court to distract you. We'll have this sorted, you'll see. We'll have *you* sorted."

Ah, lud.

"Do we have to invite *him*?" Newton muttered after his father stepped out.

Mother set her arms around him and squeezed, as she'd done so many times since he'd been a young boy. "He wants only what's best for you, dear. You'll find he's not so wrong as you currently think. He understands these things."

What Father and, unfortunately, Mother didn't understand was *him*.

Charlie did though. They'd been friends far too long and been far too honest with each other for Newton to have the least doubt on that score. Charlie would take his part. He knew he would.

Just his luck, really. He was to be assailed by his parents and championed by Cambridge's unofficial jester. This sojourn in Bath had all the markings of a miserable, frustrating, exhausting disaster.

Ellie Napper's sojourn in Bath had all the markings of a miserable, frustrating, exhausting disaster. Her family traveled to Bath at the end of each summer. Doing so allowed them the tiny nibble of Society they could afford, London being quite outside their financial means. She was joining them for the first time and discovering this visit was not meant to be a leisurely holiday.

"The seamstress I engaged is certain she can remake Lillian's gowns from last year." Mother sat at the round table in the sitting room, wire-rimmed spectacles perched at the end of her nose. "We will have to pay for new gowns for Ellie."

"Why should she have new gowns made when I have to make do with old ones?" Lillian would have struggled to sound more offended than she did.

"Believe me, I would not have chosen the arrangement," Mother said. "But we have funds enough for only one of you to have newly made gowns. And as Ellie has never left Shropshire, nothing of hers could possibly be made acceptable for Society gatherings, no matter how much effort a seamstress put into the task. And the two of you cannot share gowns, which prevents her from wearing your castoffs from last year's sojourn in Bath."

It was not a matter of embarrassment but of necessity. Lillian was reed-like. Ellie had ample curves, more than many young ladies.

"Why should the younger sister be given all the advantages of a fine seamstress?" Lillian clearly didn't mean to give over easily on the matter of their wardrobes.

"The more expensive dressmaker and the more talented one has been engaged to remake *yours*," Mother said. "We've found an adequate one to make Ellie a few acceptable gowns. She will not outshine you. Of that you can be certain."

Ellie had been certain of that even before the topic had been raised. Her family's preference for Lillian and tendency to belittle Ellie had all but guaranteed it.

Mother ran her finger down the parchment in front of her, updating Ellie and her sister, Lillian, on each item listed there. "Mrs. Clark is in Bath, as usual. We will most certainly call on her. And Mr. and Mrs. Lancaster have come also." The Lancasters were their neighbors in Shropshire, a young couple not many years older than Ellie. "With their connections, they will be the very toast of Bath. We must make certain to call on them often."

Mr. Lancaster was also on close terms with a brother of the Earl of Lampton, and he claimed both a countess and a duchess amongst his sisters.

"Will Their Graces be in Bath, do you suppose?" Lillian asked.

Mother shook her head. "Even if the duchess could convince her husband to come, they have an infant. I cannot imagine they would travel while their child is still so young."

Though Ellie was in the room, she was hardly necessary to this discussion. That was more often the case than not.

"I have heard that Lord Lampton's youngest brother is in Bath, staying with a friend of his. He will most certainly visit the Lancasters, owing to their friendship." Mother pulled off her spectacles and set them on the table, eyeing Ellie and Lillian in turn. "We must build on the progress we made when young Mr. Jonquil last visited our neighborhood. We cannot let slip by us an opportunity for a connection to that family."

"I tried, Mama," Lillian said. "He did not seem the least interested."

"Your older sister squandered her opportunity with Mr. Lancaster, preferring her penniless nobody."

The oldest Napper sister deeply loved the gentleman she had recently married, and he loved her. Beatrice was now the happiest any of them had ever seen her. But the family was meant to have been monetarily and socially benefited by the daughters' marriages. Mother was still fuming over what she considered to be Beatrice's betrayal.

"I fear you are correct about Mr. Jonquil not being persuadable toward a match with you," Mother said.

Far from looking heartbroken or offended, Lillian nodded quite matter-of-factly. She had not, after all, participated in the pursuit out of an abundance of affection.

"Mr. Jonquil's friend is Mr. Hughes, of the Sussex Hugheses. They are quite wealthy and very important." Mother held Lillian's gaze. "He would be an excellent choice."

Poor Mr. Hughes.

"And, Ellie." Mother turned her attention. "You must set your sights on Mr. Jonquil."

Poor Mr. Jonquil.

Poor me.

"If we can secure both these matches, we will be in fine feather, indeed." Mother pushed out a sigh, both worry and hope in her expression. "Your sister made a disastrous match. We cannot afford for either of you to do the same."

Ellie dreamed of a life that "disastrous."

Lillian, as always, showed no signs of hesitation. She and Mother were two peas in a pod. "How soon can we make Mr. Hughes's acquaintance?"

"I am not certain," Mother said. "We will first call on the Lancasters. That is the best initial step."

Merciful heavens, this could be a long stay in Bath.

Mother narrowed her gaze on Ellie once more. "I hope you do not plan to protest as much as you did when we were last in Mr. Jonquil's company. I know you object to the efforts needed to forge an advantageous match, but doing so is even more important than it once was."

Mother was not likely to be patient on this matter. Displeasure from her parent was not a new experience for Ellie; neither was it a pleasant one.

"I will behave," Ellie vowed.

She'd learned long ago that rebellion was pointless.

CHAPTER TWO

"I HAVE TO GET OUT of this house." Newton tossed Charlie a look of exasperation.

"But that would mean missing your father's next installment of 'Newton's Myriad Matrimonial Opportunities and the Ways in Which He Is Tossing Away His Future.' Please don't deprive me of that." A laugh twinkled in Charlie's eyes.

"Tuck the absurd grin away, Charlie. We're slipping free of our shackles whether you care to or not."

"I know the perfect place to escape to," his friend said.

"Do you?"

Charlie nodded. "Let us call on Linus."

Linus Lancaster, a former lieutenant in the Royal Navy, was something of an honorary older brother to Charlie. They'd visited the gentleman a few times since his arrival in Bath. Newton liked him and enjoyed being at his home. He and his wife were kind and wasted not a single breath lecturing Newton about his plans for the future.

"Brilliant," Newton said.

The Lancasters were letting a house near enough the Hughes's that they were able to walk there, and they did so. The day was fine, and the weather quite pleasant. Bath was bustling, as it generally was this time of year. It was, of course, nothing compared to London during the Season. Newton didn't mind the busyness. In fact, he enjoyed the constant push and pull and challenge of life in Town. He looked forward to being a more constant part of it in his own purposeful way.

"Have you found yourself a new accomplice now that I'm no longer at Cambridge?" Newton asked.

"I have, indeed." Charlie grinned. "The brother of two of my sisters-in-law, Fennel Kendrick. He finished at Eton and is coming to Cambridge at the start of term. He's always up for a lark."

"More so than I was at first?"

"*Everyone* is more up for a lark than you were," Charlie said with a laugh. "Cured you of that, though, didn't I?"

"Thoroughly."

Charlie's mischievousness had proven contagious over the years they'd known each other, and the two of them had landed in any number of scrapes. They'd not been in any significant trouble, but they'd gained a reputation for piddling bouts of mischief.

"You could always abandon your dreams of barristering and rejoin us at the ol' pile of bricks," Charlie suggested.

"*Barristering* isn't a word."

Charlie eyed him with an exaggerated expression of disapproval. "You forget yourself, sir. My brother is a most respected man of the law. That qualifies me as an expert."

"Then, apparently, you are also an expert in running an estate, breeding horses, fighting wars, and being very holy and church minded."

Charlie snorted. "Church minded is hardly the right description for me."

"Especially in the matter of Miss Sham-caster."

The only time Newton's friend audibly sighed, and not in jest, was when the topic of a certain young lady arose between them. Her name, of course, was not Sham-caster, but Lancaster. And, further, she was the youngest sister of the same Mr. Lancaster they were on their way to visit.

Newton knew he shouldn't tease his friend on this topic, but he couldn't help himself. "Miss Lancaster is an unrivaled diamond in Society. A shame she is your sworn enemy."

"Not a shame," Charlie muttered. "An inevitability."

Newton laughed ever harder. Charlie had told him endless stories of his frustrating and annoying encounters with Miss Lancaster.

"I had opportunity to interact with Miss Lancaster a few times during my brief weeks in London after Lent term. She was in Town for the Season."

"I wish you had told me of this acute and horrific suffering," Charlie said. "I would have sent you my deepest, most heartfelt sympathy, perhaps offered you safe haven with my mother."

Another laugh burst from Newton. He laughed more with Charlie than with anyone else he knew. "While I would have enjoyed spending time in your mother's company, I was not so miserable as you insist. I found Miss Lancaster far more endurable than you convinced me I would."

"Have you suffered a blow to the head?" Charlie pretended to be deeply concerned, though no one would have actually believed he was in earnest. "I can think of no other explanation for this nonsense."

Miss "Sham-caster" ruffled his even-tempered friend. How could Newton be expected not to poke at that particular nerve?

"Perhaps she has come to Bath." Newton mused over the possibility in as casual a tone as he could manage, all the while watching Charlie for a reaction.

"Bite your tongue, Hughes."

Newton laughed quietly. After a moment, Charlie laughed as well.

"Admit it," Newton said. "She's not so terrible as you describe her."

"She's not." An unexpected answer. "She's worse." Still, Charlie smiled. He didn't like Miss Lancaster—there was no doubt about that—but he was too contented a person to be truly aggravated for long.

They reached Mr. and Mrs. Lancaster's house on Lansdown Crescent. Their knock was answered quickly by a young, enthusiastic butler. The man, whose name they had learned on their first visit was Henson, was clearly new to his position and anxious to learn the way of it. Newton liked him. He was far more welcoming than the austere, staid butlers one usually encountered.

"Get on in." Henson waved them into the entryway. He caught himself. "Please come inside, gentlemen."

"Very good, man." Charlie allowed a breach of etiquette as well, slapping a hand on Henson's shoulder. "Make certain you ask for our cards."

Henson nodded. "Your cards, gentlemen?"

They handed them over.

After thinking for the length of a breath, Henson motioned to the small sitting room. "You can wait in there, I s'pose." He shook his head. "Please wait in here, gentlemen, while I see if the family is at home."

Not badly done. Henson would sort himself out soon enough. And he wasn't doing terribly, truth be told.

"Oh." Henson stopped with one foot on the staircase. "There's someone in that room. That's permissible, isn't it?"

Charlie nodded. Henson breathed a sigh of obvious relief, then hurried on his way.

Alone again, Newton spoke up, keeping his tone neutral and his laughter tucked away. "I, for one, am hoping the 'someone in this room' is a member of the extended Lancaster family."

Charlie tossed him a felling look. "Don't even joke about that."

They stepped into the room. Sitting with unmistakable grace and elegance was a young lady Newton remembered well—one did not forget a diamond of the first water.

"Mr. Jonquil," she said, her tone both painfully proper and amusingly superior. "What a . . . pleasant surprise."

"Ah, lud," Charlie muttered.

"And Mr. Hughes." She turned to him. "An actual pleasure to see you."

Newton dipped his head. "Miss Lancaster," he greeted quietly.

"My brother told me the two of you were in Bath and had called." Miss Lancaster motioned them farther into the room. Her manners could certainly not be faulted. "I had hoped you would call again."

Charlie didn't say anything. He simply stood rooted to the spot, a look of exhausted displeasure on his usually jovial face.

Newton could keep up a conversation when civility required it. "How long have you been in Bath, Miss Lancaster?"

"I arrived yesterday."

That explained why they had not yet seen her.

"When are you leaving?" Charlie muttered under his breath.

Miss Lancaster appeared to be holding back a laugh as she lowered herself into a chair. She reminded Newton of . . . well, of Charlie when he wasn't around Miss Lancaster. "My brother and his wife mean to spend another month in Bath," she said. "They have invited me to remain with them throughout their sojourn here. I intend to accept their offer."

"How fortunate for all of us," Newton said, sitting.

Miss Lancaster eyed Charlie. "Do you find it fortunate, Mr. Jonquil?"

Charlie sat as well, assuming a posture of casual disapproval. "I'd answer, but I promised my brother I wouldn't insult you anymore." He needed a moment to regain his equilibrium enough to keep that promise.

Newton far preferred silence when amongst people he did not know well, but he was not so painfully reserved as to be unable to spring to his friend's rescue. "I understand your eldest sister welcomed a new arrival a few months ago."

Miss Lancaster allowed her attention to shift to him. "She did. I have a new niece, Lady Hestia. She promises to be quite the heartbreaker, in large part because I intend to teach her well."

The amusing lady might drive Charlie rather mad, but Newton enjoyed her company. She was quick-witted and self-assured enough to not demur her way into the posture of feebleness too many young ladies were trained to assume.

Henson returned again but without the master or mistress of the house. "More visitors is about to come inside," he said.

In a quiet voice entirely lacking in mockery or jesting, Miss Lancaster said, "You simply tell us who it is by saying their names before stepping aside to allow them in."

He nodded, looking both disappointed in himself and a touch embarrassed.

"And I fear you may have forgotten to let Mr. and Mrs. Lancaster know of these gentlemen's arrival."

Henson's shoulders dropped. "I'm going to get myself tossed out of my position."

Miss Lancaster shook her head with a kind smile. "Mr. Lancaster enjoys having someone around to swap stories of the war with."

"I like that too," Henson said.

"And he has told me that he appreciates how welcome you make everyone who comes to the door."

Henson took a deep breath. "I am trying, Miss Lancaster."

"I know. And we are all so pleased."

Newton glanced at Charlie and saw precisely what he'd expected: confusion and surprise. He'd so often described Miss Sham-caster as ceaselessly shallow and self-absorbed. That description did not at all fit with the kindness she had just shown a servant who had inarguably made a mull of his most basic duties.

A knock sounded at the door. The new visitors.

Henson jumped into action, spinning about and rushing out of the sitting room.

Miss Lancaster laughed but not in derision. "He tries so very hard."

"Where did your brother find him?" Charlie asked.

She quite notably did not look at him. "Mrs. Jason Jonquil is quite an advocate for our returning war veterans. She found Henson struggling to stay afloat in the mires of London and suggested he might make a good addition to this household. Have you heard of her?"

Far from being ruffled by her teasing, fondness touched Charlie's expression. "Mariposa has single-handedly filled the staff of most London homes with one-time soldiers and sailors."

One of those former sailors popped inside a moment later and announced the newest arrivals. "Mrs. Napper." He actually counted them off on his fingers. "Miss Napper. Miss Elfrida Napper."

Charlie rose, along with Newton, as was expected, but there was exasperation in his eyes, this time not directed at Miss Lancaster.

"You are acquainted with the Nappers?" Newton asked under his breath.

"The reason I tossed myself off a roof."

Charlie had, in fact, *accidentally* fallen off a roof the year before while visiting Mr. Lancaster in Shropshire. His injuries hadn't been minor, but neither had his life been in true danger.

"You insisted Miss Lancaster was the reason you flung yourself from the vicarage."

Charlie shrugged. "I had a preponderance of reasons."

Quick introductions were exchanged as well as the requisite bows and curtsies.

Mrs. Napper's focus turned immediately to Charlie. "Mr. Jonquil. What a pleasure. You remember Lillian, of course." She pushed one of her daughters forward. "We were, of course, so honored at the friendship you two formed."

Anyone looking at Charlie could tell there was no actual friendship behind his kind, civil, silent greeting. He didn't appear to actually dislike Miss Napper, but theirs was clearly not the close connection Mrs. Napper insisted existed.

"I suspect you don't remember my younger daughter quite as well." Miss Napper pushed forward her other daughter. The older sister was all narrow lines and angles; the younger was her utter opposite. Her more curved and rounded figure softened her in a way her sister entirely lacked. "Elfrida is much quieter, much more withdrawn. A dear girl, of course, quite sweet. All the Society hostesses just adore her. But she is so demure and sweet natured that she is overlooked, I fear." Another push at the young lady's back nearly sent her tumbling to the ground. "She remembers you, of course."

"A pleasure to see you again, Miss Ellie," Charlie said.

She smiled briefly. "You remembered my preferred name."

"Of course." Charlie chose the word Mrs. Napper had used over and over again since her arrival. The Jonquils were rather famous for their wit, and the youngest of them was no different.

Mrs. Napper all but elbowed Miss Ellie toward Charlie while, in the same movement, she nudged her older daughter in Newton's direction. "Mr. Hughes, I don't believe you have met my daughter, Lillian."

Oh, lud. He was to be drawn into this? Social chatter was far from his specialty. "I have not." He dipped his head. "A pleasure, Miss Napper."

"The pleasure, I assure you, is all mine." She held his gaze a bit too anxiously.

When all the ladies were seated, Miss Napper motioned for Newton to sit beside her. Mrs. Napper repeatedly called for Charlie to sit near Miss Ellie. The young ladies' mother bore the expression of a terrier in fox-hunting season.

Charlie met Newton's eye. He raised a brow and motioned to their visitors with a look that said, "This is what I was telling you about."

Any gentleman in possession of an income and familial connections learned early how to undermine unwanted matrimonial efforts without rudeness and how to tiptoe around traps and snares. Between the unexpected presence of Charlie's sworn enemy and the pointed pursuit of the Nappers, this promised to be a most unusual sojourn in Bath.

CHAPTER THREE

The Upper Assembly Rooms in Bath held two balls each week: a Dress Ball on Monday nights and a Fancy Ball on Thursdays. Those wishing to attend could either pay for entry upon their arrival or could purchase a subscription to the Dress Balls or the Fancy Balls or both, allowing them to attend week after week. As Ellie's family could afford subscriptions to only one of the two, her parents chose the Fancy Balls, believing the addition of two cotillions to the list of dances made those gatherings more dignified.

Stepping inside the grand ballroom for their first Fancy Ball since their arrival, Ellie could not help thinking they ought to have chosen the purportedly less stately weekly gathering. Lillian's remade gowns were not in the first stare of fashion. And the gowns Mother had reluctantly agreed to have made for Ellie were rather countrified, no matter that they'd been sewn by a Bath seamstress. Their simplicity spoke not of elegance but frugality, and the indifferent workmanship rendered Ellie's appearance almost dowdy. Her appearance was hardly her only concern.

All day, all evening, all the way from their rented house to the Assembly Rooms, Ellie had been regaled with warnings and dire pronouncements regarding her expected misbehavior and embarrassments.

Do not make any of your usual impertinent remarks.

Do not be as disgracefully forward as you too often are.

Mr. Jonquil is the only prospect you have. Do not turn him away with your forwardness.

For heaven's sake, keep your peace while we are in company. Young ladies with too much to say will never be considered good company.

The list went on and on. She was fully expected to be a failure, a disgrace, an embarrassment. Her family demanded silent obedience, and she had found it best over the years to simply comply.

Her parents had enough acquaintances in Bath to be kept occupied with greetings and words of reunion for quite some time after their arrival at the ball. As this was Ellie's first time joining them, she was introduced to more people than she could possibly remember.

Their path soon crossed with the Lancasters'. The greetings were effusive on the part of Ellie's family, subdued but cordial on the part of the Lancasters. Miss Lancaster, dressed elegantly without being gaudy, offered a small smile to both Lillian and Ellie. Their acquaintance was not truly a deep one; Miss Lancaster had not lived near them for more than a decade. She traveled in much more exalted circles now.

"We were so delighted to have called yesterday and found Mr. Hughes and Mr. Jonquil there as well," Lillian said to Miss Lancaster. "They seem quite exceptional gentlemen."

"You knew Mr. Jonquil already, from his visit to Shropshire last year," Miss Lancaster said.

Lillian stumbled only a tiny bit over having been caught out pushing the topic of conversation by means of a slight misrepresentation. "Well, yes, but as he spent a vast portion of that visit convalescing, we did not spend as much time in his company as we had anticipated."

"How fortunate for you."

Only by sheer force of will did Ellie keep her amusement hidden—her family wouldn't approve of the show of levity. Miss Lancaster was clearly under no expectation of keeping quiet and outwardly reserved.

Lillian smiled conspiratorially, as if she and Miss Lancaster were the very best of friends. "You always have been so droll."

"Have I?" Miss Lancaster looked to Ellie. "Do you concur with your sister's evaluation?"

"At the moment, I find you more candid than comical."

That earned her a light laugh of what she felt certain was approval. Not everyone found a bit of wordplay off-putting.

Lillian watched them both with an expression of confusion. As she did more often than not, she turned the topic once more to the one she preferred: *her* interests. "I should very much like to make Mr. Hughes's better acquaintance. His manners yesterday were beyond reproach. His family, I understand, are the very cream of Society. One could not do better than to claim him as an acquaintance or friend."

Or more. Ellie was not unaware of her sister's ambitions.

"The Hugheses hold subscriptions to both balls," Miss Lancaster said. "I suspect he and Mr. Jonquil will both be in attendance tonight."

"Excellent." Lillian turned to Mother, the two of them conversing in low whispers.

"Has her focus shifted, then?" Miss Lancaster asked Ellie. "Mr. Jonquil seemed to be the one she had her eye on before. The one *both* of you were focused on, truth be told."

With her family's attention momentarily diverted, Ellie threw caution entirely to the wind and answered with as much candor as Miss Lancaster had earlier. "That was my parents' focus. Lillian shared the ambition. I had no choice but to act as though I did as well."

"Ah." The empathy in Miss Lancaster's expression made her less intimidating. "I did wonder why you hardly ever spoke. And if I am remembering correctly, when you did, it was mostly to echo something your sister said."

"It seemed the safest approach."

Miss Lancaster nodded. "Is that to be your approach in Bath as well?"

"In Shropshire, I had my sister's more ambitious efforts to hide behind. Here, I alone am meant to make a good showing where Mr. Jonquil is concerned." Her mother and sister were finishing their conversation, her father having stepped away, and they turned back in her direction once more. Ellie pressed her lips together and resumed her silence.

"We have just seen Mr. Hughes and Mr. Jonquil step inside," Mother said. "Come, Ellie. We must go offer our greetings."

Objections would be futile. She simply dipped her head in resignation.

To her surprise, Miss Lancaster hooked her arm through Ellie's. "Do allow me to go with you."

Lillian looked surprised. Mother could not have appeared more ecstatic.

"If I am not mistaken," Ellie said, "you do not overly care for Mr. Jonquil."

"No, but I am terribly fond of the theater, and we are about to be treated to quite a performance."

Again, Ellie barely managed to hold back her amusement. If Mother's gaze had not been unwaveringly focused on the gentlemen ahead of them, she would have scolded Ellie to no end.

"I only wish I didn't have to be one of the performers," Ellie said.

"Stick close to me. I'll do what I can to extricate you."

It was, quite possibly, the most generous and welcome offer she had received in years. "Thank you, Miss Lancaster."

"Call me Artemis," she said. "We cannot be allies if we aren't friends."

"I would be honored to be either one."

"Why not both?" So many of the fashionable and sought-after young ladies in Society were rumored to be quite above their company, looking down their noses at those who did not claim the standing and wealth they did. Artemis was proving quite the opposite.

They were soon standing before Mr. Hughes and Mr. Jonquil. Bows and curtsies and words of delighted welcome were exchanged, the more effusive of it coming from Mother and Lillian.

"A delight to see you again, Miss Lancaster." Mr. Jonquil's greeting was not impolite, but neither did it seem entirely sincere. They neither of them seemed overly fond of the other, yet there was no real animosity apparent.

"Of course it is." She shrugged a shoulder, then turned with cool confidence to the other gentleman. "You have had my deepest empathy these past days, Mr. Hughes."

"Why is that?" He spoke as quietly as he had the day before, not in a tone of true bashfulness but as someone who was simply more contemplative and reserved.

"One cannot be subjected to Mr. Jonquil's company without suffering greatly in the enduring of it."

Mr. Hughes did not appear to take her entirely seriously. Mr. Jonquil looked as though he very much wished to object to Artemis's declaration but didn't care to make a scene.

Mother opened her mouth, no doubt wishing to direct the conversation, but Artemis spoke too quickly.

"Miss Ellie and I have been enjoying a very convivial conversation, but I have learned that she has not yet been engaged for the next set."

Like a magpie in pursuit of the next shiny treasure, Mother seized the moment. "Lillian is not yet engaged either. Mr. Hughes, would you be so good as to fill the gap?"

If he was overly shocked at the breach of etiquette—gentlemen were seldom pressed so directly—he did not indicate as much. He simply dipped his head without the slightest change to his expression. Ellie hadn't the first idea whether he was humorless or stern. Perhaps both. She didn't dislike him; she simply didn't know what to make of him.

"And, Mr. Jonquil," Mother pressed forward. "Elfrida is unlikely to secure a partner if you do not show her a degree of compassion." She had secured

Lillian a partner without actually insulting her. Ellie never did seem to warrant consideration.

"I doubt she could be here long without being quite in demand." Mr. Jonquil turned to Ellie. "Might I secure your company for the next set before someone else swoops in and snatches you away?"

Though she did not intend to cooperate enough with her parents' dictates to actually try ensnaring Mr. Jonquil, she was deeply grateful to him for that moment of kindness. He had salvaged her dignity and had done so without drawing undue attention.

Ample time remained before the next set would begin for all the parties involved to spend a little more time interacting with others. The gentlemen, no doubt, planned on doing precisely that. But Lillian kept close to Mr. Hughes's side, not so subtly reaching for his arm and all but forcing him to offer it to her. She smiled up at him, not in pleasure but in something far more like victory.

"I cannot imagine you do not remember that look," Ellie said quietly to Mr. Jonquil.

"It haunts my dreams." His tone was teasing, but his words were sincere. "I will drop a word of warning into my friend's ear, assuming he is able to eventually slip free."

She offered him an apologetic glance. "I hope he will not think too poorly of my family. I also hope he will take your warning seriously."

"His is a compassionate nature and a remarkable intellect," Mr. Jonquil said. "He'll be wise in both regards."

Ellie remained in the grouping, knowing her mother would allow nothing else. As dictated by her family, she kept very quiet. As dictated by her own integrity, she kept a physical distance from the gentleman they meant for her to pursue.

Lillian offered Mr. Hughes no such reprieve. By the time the next set was over and the two gentlemen returned them to their parents, the poor soul looked ready to run for his life. What little subtlety Lillian had employed during their efforts in Shropshire had yet to make an appearance here.

If they were not all very careful, Lillian's efforts might just prove successful. And if she managed to ensnare her chosen prey, Ellie would be under increasing pressure to capture the quarry chosen for her.

And they would all live unhappily ever after.

CHAPTER FOUR

IF NOT FOR THE VERY real possibility that Miss Napper would drag him quite literally to the altar should he offer her even the tiniest encouragement, Newton would have faced the remainder of his time in Bath with equanimity. The Nappers were not objectionable by Society's standards, but Newton had no desire to entangle himself. He already felt trapped enough by his parents' dictates and demands.

"We have been invited to take supper and spend an evening with Mr. and Mrs. Lancaster," Mother said. The three of them—Newton and both of his parents—were making what was proving to be a biweekly visit to the Grand Pump Room to walk and, in Mother's case, to take the waters. Charlie, intelligent chap that he was, never joined them.

"An excellent connection, there," Father said. "And that Miss Lancaster would be quite a feather in your quiver."

"I beg your pardon?"

Father quickly realized the potential insult in the metaphor. "I hadn't meant to be demeaning. Her standing in Society is second to none. That you can claim her as a friend will serve to elevate your standing. The possibility of something more is quite encouraging."

Light spilled in through the windows, brightly illuminating the space, in stark contrast to Newton's dark and dreary mood as he discussed the current matter. His parents understood so little of what he wished for in life. "I am not interested in 'something more.'"

Mother patted his arm. "Perhaps not at this exact moment. But do keep your mind open to the possibility. She is a lovely young lady and precisely the sort we would wish for you."

Countless arguments immediately rose to mind. He knew better than to voice them. His parents had set their sights on more than just his future occupation—or the blocking of it, more accurately. They were also being dictatorial in the matter of his future spouse. It was a difficult thing to be so little understood.

"If I will not be needed," he said, "I believe I will take a turn about the room on my own. The space is a peaceful one."

That was something of a lie. Though Bath was not as highly sought-after a city as it had been mere years earlier, it was still popular enough for the Grand Pump Room to be fuller than Newton would have preferred. In that moment, though, he knew himself more equal to enduring the press of strangers than his parents' intrusion.

Mother nodded. "Take a turn, Newton. I mean to make slow work of the waters today."

He did not need to be told twice.

A half circuit of the long, high-ceilinged room brought him, to his great surprise, face-to-face with Miss Lancaster and Miss Ellie Napper. He attempted to offer a quick nod and be on his way, but it was not to be.

"We'd hoped to find you here," Miss Lancaster said. "We are hatching a wonderfully clever scheme, and we need you to join in our conspiracy if we are to have any hope of success."

He was at an utter loss for a reply. They wished him to join in a plot? He hadn't a long-standing association with either young lady, and neither did he suspect he'd given either one the impression that he was a likely candidate for group mischief.

"At least hear us out," Miss Lancaster pleaded.

He could see no means of escaping their explanation. It might even prove a little diverting. The heavens knew he could use a bit of lightening after his difficult interactions with his parents.

He gave a slight nod.

A grin spread across Miss Lancaster's face. "Excellent."

Newton took a moment to study Miss Ellie. He couldn't imagine her undertaking anything remotely likely to raise eyebrows. To his utter shock, he saw as much mischief in her eyes as he did in her companion's. Entirely unexpected.

"Let us continue our walk around the room," Miss Lancaster suggested. "We will make you privy to the details of our plot." She slipped her hand into the crook of his arm, not requiring him to offer it. He did, however, undertake the niceties with Miss Ellie and, in the length of a breath, had a young lady on each arm as he resumed his walk around the Pump Room. It was an odd posture for one who tended toward quiet solitude or membership in the crowd of onlookers rather than the out-and-outers. Still, he was not complaining.

"Here is our situation." It was Miss Ellie and not Miss Lancaster who began the telling. "My parents are single-mindedly determined to see me make a match with Mr. Jonquil, which I don't particularly care to pursue."

"No intelligent person would," Miss Lancaster tossed in.

"And my sister is equally determined to pursue *you*, Mr. Hughes," Miss Ellie said. "Unless I entirely misread the situation, you are not particularly keen on that."

This was not the demure, quiet miss he'd interacted with thus far. There was a boldness to her no one would predict.

"Have I misunderstood your feelings for my sister?" Miss Ellie pressed.

"You have not."

Far from offended on her sister's behalf, Miss Ellie nodded. "I suspected as much. It seems the four of us are in something of a bind."

"The *five* of us," Newton corrected, drawing both their attention fully to him. "My father has latched on to the idea that Miss Lancaster would make me an excellent wife."

Miss Lancaster snorted. "We would be terribly ill-suited."

Indeed, they would. Newton enjoyed what he knew of Miss Lancaster, but he knew he would find her utterly exhausting were they to attempt to build any sort of life together.

"Our plan is even more ingenious than we realized." Miss Ellie leaned the tiniest bit forward and addressed her remark across him to Miss Lancaster. "It will rescue you as well."

His curiosity was thoroughly piqued but not the least satisfied. Part of him wondered how essential he actually was to this plan if they had already declared it a roaring success without informing him of any part of it.

"We would like to recruit you for a vague and entirely fabricated courtship." Miss Ellie's eyes shone with merriment and mischief. "Nothing pointed, nothing that would cause whispers or raise expectations, but enough time and attention that my parents would not push me to throw myself at Charlie and my sister would relax her efforts in your direction."

That would certainly be an improvement.

"And, Mr. Hughes," Miss Lancaster joined the explanation, "seeing your interest directed elsewhere might convince your parents not to push you to pursue anything but a friendly connection to me."

He did like the escape they were offering, but his misgivings were plentiful. "This would require remarkable care. Should expectations be raised . . ."

"We have thought of that," Miss Ellie said. Heavens, she was actually bouncing a little. The humdrum young lady he'd encountered at the ball had disappeared entirely, replaced by, if he did not miss his mark, one as capable of legendary mischief as Charlie in his Eton days. "If most of our time together, the two of us, is spent in the company of both Artemis and Mr. Jonquil, then people will never be entirely certain if our connection is truly a budding courtship or simply an extension of the four of us being friends."

The four *of us?* Newton looked to Miss Lancaster. "Charlie has agreed to participate?"

"He has."

"And does he know that—?" A careful tone seemed best when on such thin ice. "Is he aware *you* are part of the scheme?"

She grinned. "That did give him pause. But in the end, his wish to not see you miserable outweighed his utterly nonsensical animosity toward me."

"You do enjoy poking at him," Newton pointed out.

She pressed her free hand to her heart in a show of feigned innocence. "I would never do any such thing."

"That is precisely the expert acting we will need if we are to be successful in this scheme," Miss Ellie said.

"I am ready to dedicate myself to this absurdly entertaining venture," Miss Lancaster said. "Will you take up the cause, Mr. Hughes?"

With this scheme, he could avoid Miss Napper's trap, assist in Charlie's escape from a similar situation, and perhaps loosen his parents' grip on his future. "I believe I shall."

"Excellent." Miss Lancaster pulled her arm from his. "I am going to go speak a moment with Miss Carlton—she is a dear friend, one of a few here in Bath just now. The two of you continue your circuit of the room, and I will rejoin you after a time."

Newton understood the strategy: he and Miss Ellie would be seen in each other's company—exclusive company for a brief time—which would begin to lay the foundation of the ruse they were enacting without being the least shocking or inappropriate.

Miss Lancaster slipped away.

"She is a whirlwind, is she not?" Miss Ellie said.

Newton kept an eye on the crowd around them, not wishing to cause a collision, but also watched Miss Ellie more closely. There was a time for silence and a time for speaking up. The current moment called for the latter. "Please be fully honest with me, Miss Ellie. Do you truly wish to undertake this campaign? I would not want you to be bullied into anything of which you are not truly in favor."

"I assure you, I am not being pressured into participation. Artemis and I hatched this scheme *together*."

She was quite full of surprises. Newton's interactions with her up until this one had given the impression of an almost excessively prim young lady, one who would most certainly not whip up a plan for a feigned courtship. "And you are not bothered by the deception, Miss Ellie?"

"Is not Society's matrimonial dance one of deception?" she asked. "We are, at least, choosing to be honest with each other, something few would-be couples bother with."

There was a great deal of truth in that.

"If we are to be co-conspirators," she continued on, "I would welcome your use of my Christian name. Perhaps not in public—a scandal being a vastly different thing than a mere distraction—but at least when we are scheming together."

He sketched the tiniest bow, one likely a bit too formal for the decidedly informal conversation they were undertaking. "Very well, Ellie."

"I do not know your Christian name," she said.

He was agreeing to a most unusual arrangement with a young lady he knew so little that even his given name was a mystery to her. It was utterly out of character for him. Yet, he pressed on. "Newton."

"I do not believe I've known anyone whose given name was Newton. It is unique without being . . . odd."

He nodded. "I am not displeased with it."

"I do not feel that way about *my* Christian name, I assure you. It is both unusual and strange, and I do not like it at all."

"Hence your preference for Ellie."

"More than preference. Insistence." She looked up at him.

He had always liked brown eyes; he liked hers. "I will, of course, make certain to abide by that insistence."

She bit back a grin. "I cannot imagine you did not notice how frequently my mother employs that phrase."

"Of course I did."

Her smile blossomed, her eyes dancing and sparkling. He had not expected to form an alliance with any young lady, but he was actually looking forward to the diversion this would no doubt prove to be: an unpredictable and excessively interesting lark.

CHAPTER FIVE

To Ellie's delight, Artemis called the next day. She did not arrive alone but with two fashionable, distinguished young ladies their same age. Mother was too in awe to do anything but sit and watch them wide-eyed. Lillian sat among them as well, inserting herself into the conversation as often as possible. None of their visitors was the least bit rude or unkind, but no one could possibly think Lillian was the reason they had come to call.

"Do say you will join our little band for the Dress Ball at the Upper Assembly Rooms on Monday," Miss Mullins said. "We have such larks when we are together at Society functions."

The offer was directed to Ellie, *exclusively* to Ellie. Lillian was clearly not pleased. Mother, however, watched and listened with delight.

"Might I attend with them?" Ellie asked, having maintained the demure aura her mother required, all the while nearly overwhelmed with excitement. She had longed for friends. Dreamed of having them. And here they were.

"We only have a subscription to the Fancy Balls," Mother reminded her in a tight whisper.

"That is an easily rectified impediment." Artemis spoke with the confidence only Society's sweetheart could claim. "I have a subscription to both, and my Dress Ball subscription includes two transferable tickets. My brother allows me the choosing of who receives those."

"*Two?*" Lillian asked, her tone both pointed and excessively innocent.

"That is the established number." Artemis left her explanation at that, avoiding the invitation everyone must have known Lillian was angling for.

"We mean to promenade along the Gravel Walk," Miss Phelps said. She was quieter than her two friends but just as personable. "Will you come with us?"

"Do," Artemis said, her tone conspiratorial. "We might cross paths with Mr. Hughes."

That perked Lillian up on the instant. "Truly?"

Artemis gave her a cursory nod but kept her attention on Ellie. "He told me he enjoyed your brief conversation yesterday at the Pump Room."

"I enjoyed his company as well." It wasn't a lie—he was amiable, and she hadn't disliked their interaction. But it had been too brief for her to have truly formed an opinion of him. Still, she knew the role she was meant to play. "Will he be at the Dress Ball also, do you suppose?"

Miss Mullins nodded. "As will Mr. Charlie Jonquil." She traded looks with Miss Phelps. "So, so handsome."

Artemis held her peace because no one else shared her opinion of Mr. Jonquil.

"Have you ever seen all seven of the Jonquil brothers together?" Miss Mullins flipped open her fan and flicked it back and forth, creating a quick, utilitarian breeze. "No woman should be expected to form a coherent thought when faced with so overwhelmingly beautiful a sight as that."

Mother found her voice at last. "Will he be on the Gravel Walk this afternoon, do you suppose? I have hoped our Ellie might make his better acquaintance."

"He and Mr. Hughes are friends," Artemis said. "They may very well be together."

Ellie began to say something that might move her mother's thoughts away from Mr. Jonquil, but a subtle shake of Artemis's head told her not to.

"We had best make our way there," Miss Mullins said. "Do come, Ellie."

Ellie looked to her mother and received permission.

"Do not forget yourself and become disagreeable or forward," Mother whispered as Ellie passed. "And do what you can to speak of your sister to Mr. Hughes without it seeming pointed or forced."

Ellie nodded, though she didn't intend to do any such thing.

"And attempt to claim at least a moment of Mr. Jonquil's attention, despite his . . . options in this group."

Ellie offered another disingenuous nod and hurried after her new friends, slipping happily from the house.

"How did we do, Artemis?" Miss Phelps asked.

"Brilliantly," she said. "Even if you did go on and on in that ridiculous fashion about Charlie Jonquil."

Miss Mullins and Miss Phelps exchanged delighted looks with Ellie. They obviously found Artemis's enmity entertaining.

They walked in a clump in the direction of the Gravel Walk. It was a fashionable place to be seen. Ellie had been there once on this trip to Bath, but as she had undertaken the jaunt with her mother and sister, they had not precisely made a splash.

"Artemis told us about your scheme," Miss Mullins said. "I do hope you will allow us to join in the diversion. I believe you will find we are excellent co-conspirators."

"I would be delighted to have you join in, Miss Mullins. And you too, of course, Miss Phelps."

Artemis laughed. "There's none of that Miss So-and-So amongst us. The Huntresses are on a Christian-name basis."

"Huntresses?"

Artemis nodded quite solemnly. "My ancient namesake had a band of huntresses, and they were absolutely everything young ladies ought to be permitted to be: fierce, strong, capable, and entirely in control of their own destinies. We mean to emulate them in every way possible."

"Including the part where they murder people who sneak into their ranks unwelcome?" Ellie asked.

"Especially that part," Artemis said with a grin.

Ellie did not actually think they meant to murder anyone. But their fearless leader clearly found the comparison entertaining.

"Miss Phelps is Gillian," Artemis said. "And Miss Mullins is Daria."

"Ellie," she said to them both.

They walked on, reaching the Gravel Walk at last. The tree-strewn path was far from empty. Strolling about with these three fashionable young ladies made her far more the center of attention than she was accustomed to being.

Lillian would be in a fury if she could see her younger sister meandering along the shaded walk, being looked at with admiration while she herself had been denied the opportunity. When Lillian was denied the things she wished for, she could have something of a temper. Ellie didn't wish for Mr. Hughes to be cornered into a match that would render him at the mercy of an unpredictable and, at times, unpleasant disposition. He was personable, kind, and so quiet. What a mismatch that would be.

"Now, our difficulty is attempting to spot the two gentlemen we are hoping to see," Gillian said.

Daria had an easy answer for that. "We simply pay attention to which direction every lady's eye turns. That would undoubtedly lead us to Mr. Jonquil, and Mr. Hughes will most certainly be with him. Easy as can be."

Though Artemis appeared a bit annoyed at the rationale, she did not argue with the strategy. Mere moments later, it proved ingenious. Heads were indeed turning as Mr. Jonquil ambled along. Ellie had met only one of his older brothers—the earl—when he had come to the little neighborhood for Mr. and Mrs. Lancaster's wedding. He was very fine looking as well. She could only imagine the effects of seven such attractive gentlemen all gathered together.

Mr. Hughes was perhaps not as stunningly handsome, but he was quite pleasant in his own way. Quiet, subdued, with the look of one who listened closely and pondered deeply. He was less stately than many gentlemen of the *ton*. He was also less overwhelming. That would make their ruse far easier to manage.

The two gentlemen greeted all four of them with the appropriate bows and words of welcome.

"I see the Huntresses have re-formed here in Bath." Mr. Hughes looked to Charlie and explained. "Miss Lancaster and her cohorts are quite famous in Town."

"*In*famous?" Charlie spoke the incorrect echo with a look of feigned innocence.

Artemis did not rise to the bait but simply stood and waited.

Charlie turned his attention to Ellie. "Have you been conscripted, Miss Ellie?"

"I have joined the brigade willingly," she said. "Unlike Mr. Hughes, who was most certainly conscripted."

Newton smiled a little, more than he usually did but less obviously than most people. "My participation is entirely willing as well."

"And are you terrified?" She allowed her enjoyment of their slightly absurd conversation to show, something she never permitted. Something *her mother* never permitted.

"On the contrary," he said. "I find myself increasingly delighted."

Ellie enjoyed being able to speak so openly and genuinely with someone without having to hide behind the facade her mother had invented for her. During the time she spent with Newton, she would be permitted the freedom to be herself in a way she seldom was.

The group continued on, Daria walking beside Charlie, Artemis and Gillian forming a second grouping, and Ellie and Newton walking side-by-side.

"If we are to make our scheme believable," Newton said, "we would be well advised to learn a little about each other."

"I agree," Ellie said.

"What would you like to know about me?" he asked.

Ellie didn't have a ready answer. Young ladies were not permitted to be so forward as that. Mother's warning echoed in her ears, but she pushed it aside. Worrying about disobeying Mother on that matter seemed rather ridiculous when she was disobeying in a much larger way.

"Allow me to begin," Newton said. "It may be easier that way."

Ellie nodded her agreement. They passed under a particularly large tree, its expansive branches creating a pattern of dappled light on everything beneath it.

"How old are you?" Newton asked.

Ellie found she could almost laugh. It was such basic information, yet they didn't know that about each other. "I am nearly nineteen."

"I am recently turned twenty-one," he said. "I have also recently finished my time in Cambridge."

"I am afraid I cannot claim an alma mater," Ellie said. "I did attempt to slip past the gates of Oxford and gain entry, but it seems my dress and bonnet gave me away. I was tossed out quite unceremoniously."

Far from being horrified at her ridiculousness, Newton laughed. The laughter did her a world of good. Comments such as the one she had just made had earned her any number of punishments and lectures from her parents. He, however, seemed to appreciate her.

"And what do you mean to do now that you have finished your time at University?" Ellie asked.

"That depends entirely upon whom you ask."

"Do you always answer questions with riddles?"

He smiled, again that barely discernible smile. "The sad result of not enough practice, I suppose."

"I have noticed your tendency to keep your peace," she said.

A little hesitation entered his expression. "Do you consider such to be a failing?"

She adjusted her arm, set in the crook of his, so she walked a touch closer. "Not a failing at all."

He did not speak again for several long moments, but it was not an uncomfortable silence nor an offended one. Though nothing about him changed outwardly, Ellie felt certain he was more relaxed, more at ease.

"What are these varying views on your post-University pursuits?" she asked.

"My father is determined that I will be a gentleman of leisure, whiling away my life with overtly gentlemanly pursuits and living off the wealth he has so carefully guarded and accumulated."

There was one opinion from one parent. "And according to your mother?"

"I will marry a young lady of tremendous standing in Society—at the moment, she is in agreement with my father's choice of Miss Lancaster—and then proceed to those very gentlemanly pursuits."

Ellie stepped carefully around a partially protruding tree root in the path. "Your mother will realize my family claims an insignificant place in Society, and with a little effort, she will come to know just how minuscule my dowry is. Will this ruse we are enacting cause you a great deal of difficulty?"

"I am not inexperienced with the 'difficulty' inherent in being lectured by my parents. I assure you, I can endure it again."

"My mother is fond of lecturing as well," she said. "While my father doesn't participate, he also does not ever defend me."

Newton set his hand atop hers. "I am sorry to hear that."

She didn't know how much of the kind gesture was sincere and how much was for the benefit of those watching—they were co-conspirators in a plot, after all—but she was grateful, just the same. Enduring her mother's dictates and demands and her father's complacency had been a lonely burden.

"You have not addressed the matter of what you wish to do with your life now that you've finished at Cambridge." What would *his* thoughts on the matter be?

"If I had my way, I would immediately attach myself to an Inn of Court and study the law in order to pursue a career as a barrister."

She could easily picture him acting in that role. His appeared to be a methodical mind, and heaven knew he possessed a calm and deliberate demeanor. "Your parents object to this plan?"

"Quite vociferously."

"Parents are such a painful form of torture at times," she said. "They are forever placing a person in the untenable position of deciding between being true to oneself and keeping the peace."

"And it is an uncomfortable outcome either way."

They walked on awhile. He did not demand conversation nor agreement. He did not look down on her for behaving in a more forceful manner than her parents were comfortable with. And he was kind. Of all the people Artemis might've suggested she could pretend to be courted by, he was proving a good choice.

She began to believe she just might survive this stay in Bath.

Barely.

CHAPTER SIX

"Unfortunately, my sister-in-law is a decent person." Artemis rolled her eyes with the theatrical air that Newton had discovered was near constant with her. She turned to Charlie standing nearby and held up a single finger as if to scold him. "Not a word from you, Charles."

Charlie held up his hands in a show of feigned innocence. These two never stopped nipping at each other. Newton found it simultaneously entertaining and a little tiring.

Artemis continued. "Despite my pleadings, my uncooperative family has invited the Nappers to this evening's gathering. I, being the intelligent one, suggested we limit the invitation to only Ellie."

The two young ladies had become fast friends. Newton could understand why. Artemis was a lark. Ellie was a joy.

"Lillian will be here," Artemis said, "which will likely make things a little uncomfortable for you, Newton. I don't doubt you know how to navigate this particular quagmire, but I regret that you have to."

"Is that not the reason for our scheme?"

Artemis smiled mischievously. "Oh yes. I haven't the least doubt it will help, but we are so early in our plan that the scheme will not do you as much good as it will in a few more weeks."

Newton nodded, not overly worried.

"Mr. Napper is relatively harmless but only because he is relatively uninvolved this time. He had plenty to say when Lillian was pursuing"—her eyes darted to Charlie—"less exalted options."

"No argument from me," Charlie said. "Newton's a far better catch than I'll ever be."

"Truer words were never spoken." Artemis turned once more to Newton. "Mr. Napper will cause you few headaches. *Mrs.* Napper is another matter entirely."

"She's not likely to be put off the scent?"

Artemis shook her head. "We can certainly outsmart her on that score. I worry far more about her treatment of Ellie. Mrs. Napper is not kind to her. And when Ellie is in company with her mother, she's a different person: coerced into near silence, withdrawn in a way that speaks of duress."

"Is that why she was so different during our promenade yesterday than she was at the Fancy Ball?" Charlie asked. "I found the change in her confusing."

Artemis sighed. "The Nappers were our neighbors when I still lived in the Lancaster family home. I didn't know Lillian and Ellie well then—I moved away when I was still quite young—but on all of my visits since, I have found myself utterly exasperated with Mrs. Napper. Parents ought not despise the person their child is, but she has always seemed to dislike Ellie, or at least *disapprove* of her."

"That is, unfortunately, not an uncommon affliction." Newton knew all too well how it felt to have one's parents wish he were different than he actually was.

"Would we do best to speak on her behalf or ignore it?" Charlie asked. "I wouldn't wish to make things worse for Miss Ellie. But listening to a lady being harangued and not stepping in goes entirely against my nature."

Newton smiled at his friend. "You Jonquils never can resist helping someone in need."

"A trait I inherited from my father."

"I've met your mother," Newton said. "I can say with absolute certainty that you inherited that from her as well."

Charlie smiled fondly and, if Newton didn't miss his mark, a little sadly. Charlie longed for his mother's company when he was away from home, though he had been loath to admit it while they were still at school. The other boys had taken great delight in teasing him over his deep attachment to his mother during their years at Eton. However, few of them understood the enormous pain he felt at having lost his father before he'd even begun his first year there.

Artemis's expression had also softened. She knew Charlie's mother, after all. No one who had ever met the Dowager Countess of Lampton felt anything but deep admiration for her, and she treated everyone with sincere kindness.

Mr. Lancaster stepped into the drawing room. He bore a striking resemblance to his younger sister, both boasting golden curls and startlingly green eyes. He was also every bit as witty and quick with a jest as she was. Newton had enjoyed coming to know them both. He enjoyed their company better than his own parents'.

"Henson tells me our guests are beginning to arrive," Mr. Lancaster said.

"Oh, how I wish I'd been present to hear *how* he told you," Artemis said.

Mr. Lancaster laughed. "He regularly sends my Arabella into fits of laughter, though I suspect he doesn't mean to. I'll keep him on forever if it means seeing her so happy."

Newton dreamed of a marriage like theirs, built on love and adoration and mutual happiness. How could his parents not want that for him?

Newton's parents arrived within the next few minutes, followed by the Nappers and the Mullins. That, as it turned out, was the extent of the guest list. Mother was quite felicitous toward Artemis. Mrs. Napper worked herself into something of a frenzy attempting to show equal attention to both Charlie and Newton. The elder Miss Napper never seemed more than a few feet away from him. And Artemis did her utmost to slip free of his mother and pull him and Ellie near enough for conversation and interaction.

It was the most ridiculous dance.

Charlie, of all people, proved the most adept. After nearly an hour, he announced to the gathering "an excellent idea" for making the most of the evening. "Those of us unattached and without wisdom wrought from life experience"—he motioned subtly with his head toward the older, married set—"would feel simply awful if we disrupted the, no doubt, important conversations occurring around us. Might I suggest that Miss Lancaster, Mr. Hughes, the Misses Napper, the younger Mr. Mullins, Miss Mullins, and I form our own little party and take up a parlor game?"

An excellent idea, indeed.

Artemis wasted not a moment grasping the opportunity. "Oh, please, could we play short answer?"

Charlie shrugged, apparently not overly worried about *which* game was chosen. Artemis's suggestion was taken up by the others. Short answer was a relatively simply game but a challenging one, just the same. Each participant would, in turn, ask a question, and the person to his or her right would be required to answer it in a single syllable. No one was permitted to ask a question already posed nor choose an answer already given.

They were soon situated on one side of the drawing room, occupying chairs gathered in a circle. If not for the Mullins siblings—Tobias and Daria—they would never have managed to arrange the seven of them such that no one was seated beside the person who was being thrust upon them by well-meaning parents while still making certain Newton and Ellie sat beside one another. The arrangement would help with the impression they were trying to make, but Newton also looked forward to watching her play this fast-paced game of quick answers and witty questions. The Ellie he'd met at the Fancy Ball would have been rubbish at it. The Ellie who'd persuaded him to take part in her plot would likely triumph over them all.

"What will be the forfeit for a participant whose answer breaks the rules?" Miss Napper asked.

"Elimination," Artemis said. "For that particular round, at least. We will narrow down the participants until we have a champion of each round. The person who is champion the most will be declared monarch of the evening."

"Monarch?" Ellie grinned. "I hope that comes with an unhealthy degree of unmitigated power."

"Ellie, do show some decorum," Miss Napper said quietly but not quietly enough. The circle was small. No one was far from anyone else.

"I suggest Miss Lancaster begin," Tobias said. "The game was her suggestion."

Artemis accepted the invitation with an eager grace. She turned to Charlie. "Which county is your favorite?"

A difficult question to answer according to the rules. Were there any counties in the kingdom that had one-syllable names? Newton's mind spun, trying to remember them all.

With no more than a moment's thought, Charlie answered. "Kent." He, then, turned to Daria. "What sort of evening are we having tonight?"

"Grand," Daria answered quickly.

Charlie smiled at her, apparently pleased to have not bested her. Daria, blushing more than a little, turned her attention to Newton, who sat at her right. "When, sir, do you think is the best time to pose a difficult question?"

"Now." He turned to Ellie with a grin. She, diverting lady that she was, made a show of being nervous. "Pray, Miss Ellie, how do you fare this evening?"

With an arching of her eyebrow, she said, "Fair." Excellent wordplay.

She turned to her sister, the next to receive a question. "Which dance do you dance best?"

Lillian's eyes darted about as she thought. She needed a few moments but managed an answer relatively quickly. "Reel."

As Lillian turned to Tobias to pose her question, Ellie leaned toward Newton. "I was so hoping she would stumble on waltz first and blurt that out before she could stop herself."

The waltz was quite new and, as it was danced with the gentleman's arm wrapped rather intimately around the lady's middle, was considered scandalous. Newton came surprisingly close to laughing, something he seldom did in company.

By the time the game had wound its way back to Newton, Daria had been eliminated.

Newton knew the perfect question to pose to Ellie. "Which dance would you be most likely to offer to teach a stranger?"

Charlie and Artemis laughed out loud. Ellie grinned. He had caught her in the very trap she'd set for her sister. This time, though, she could not give "reel" as an answer; that answer had already been used.

She, however, was not the least rattled. "None."

Oh, she was clever.

Ellie turned to Lillian. "Which of the Jonquil brothers is the most handsome?"

Newton pressed his lips closed to hold back a grin. None of the brothers had a one-syllable name, and Lillian could not answer "None," as Ellie had already used that response. "All" would be a workable answer, but Lillian would likely worry that she would give offense to Charlie. The answers were not meant to be necessarily correct, simply possible. And, of course, quite short.

Lillian's expression turned quickly from ponderous to frustrated and defensive. "That is an unfair question. It cannot be answered, as you are well aware."

"I believe you have exceeded the syllable limit." Ellie's tone was merry but not mocking.

Her sister only grew more upset.

Charlie jumped to the rescue. "You can rejoin in the next round," he said kindly. "Perhaps we'll ask questions in the other direction, and you can ask a question your sister cannot answer."

Despite having been offered a means of keeping her dignity intact, Lillian simply sat in unhappy silence.

One by one, everyone was eliminated except for Newton and Ellie. For the first time, *she* posed a question to *him*. "If you hadn't a rose near to hand, which flower would you offer a young lady?"

A one-syllable flower. But not a rose. He could think of any number of plants, even flowering trees, but no true flowers. He could not say "None" or "All," both having been used already.

Ellie watched him with dancing, happy eyes. She was so clearly enjoying herself. This glimpse of the *real* Ellie was delightful. Utterly so.

If he hadn't roses near to hand, which flower would he offer her?

"Whichever flower she prefers."

Though the answer lost him the game, it gained him a sweet and appreciative smile, one he hoped to see again.

The evening continued on, and the group played game after game of short answer. The undertaking was filled with laughter and teasing, clever questions, and equally clever answers. Only once was Newton able to outwit Ellie, while she caught him out twice. More impressive still, she managed once to confound Charlie, and Newton had never met that man's intellectual equal.

The more he learned of Ellie Napper, the more he liked her.

CHAPTER SEVEN

"WHILE I HATE TO ADMIT that Artemis is correct about anything," Charlie said, "her strategy for today is bang on. We'd do best to stick to it."

Newton nodded. They were on their way to call on the Napper sisters. Charlie, who had been designated by Ellie's parents as their choice for her, would show equal and neutral attention to both ladies. Newton, who had been selected for Lillian, would give notably more attention to Ellie while not giving the impression of an active, determined courtship. It was a narrow ledge to navigate but one that would save all of them a great deal of misery if they managed it.

Their knock was answered by a staid and respectable butler. Today was the Napper ladies' at-home day, and thus, Charlie and Newton were not required to wait to see how their cards were received. They were ushered into the drawing room, where a small gathering of ladies—young, old, and otherwise—were conversing reservedly.

Mrs. Napper welcomed them with a mixture of enthusiasm and almost painful decorum. "Do come sit with the girls." She motioned the both of them to chairs near her daughters.

Newton moved directly to the one nearest Ellie, but Mrs. Napper stopped him.

"You are welcome to sit here, Mr. Hughes." She indicated a seat closer to Lillian.

"I thank you," he said, "but I would not wish to give Miss Ellie the impression that I do not wish to take the seat I was aiming for, as that would seem a slight against her. No gentleman would wish to so mistreat a lady."

Her mother clearly wasn't certain how to contradict that.

Ellie spoke up. "You are so kind, Mr. Hughes. Thank you for sparing my feelings. I would, of course, be honored to have you sit near me."

He dipped his head. "The honor is all mine, Miss Ellie."

Newton caught Charlie's eye as he lowered himself into the chair. Had he done too much? Ought he not to have offered so much praise or been so vocal about sitting next to her in particular? But Charlie nodded subtly, encouragingly.

They were all situated, and the conversations around the room resumed. Ellie turned to Newton almost immediately. "I've thought of an answer to the one question you baffled me with during the games of short answer."

She had stumbled over only one of the questions he'd asked her during that game: *Which of the King's children is most pleasant?* It had been both a bit tongue-in-cheek, requiring that she imply the other princes and princesses were poor company, and all but impossible to answer. "George" had been given as an answer already in that round, and none of the others had one-syllable Christian names. "Kent" and "York" had also been used, eliminating her ability to refer to those of the children whose titles were but one syllable. The usual fallbacks—"none," "all," etc.—had also been unavailable.

"And what answer have you to give now?" he asked, truly intrigued.

"*Tous.*"

For just a moment, he wasn't certain what she'd said. But then the genius of it became clear. "*Tous,*" he repeated. "French for 'all.'"

She smiled broadly, a laugh in her eyes. "Once I realized we had not specifically barred answers already given in English if given in another language, the answer became clear."

"You've been pondering this ever since being denied victory?"

"I'm not Napoleon; I do not surrender."

It was all he could do not to laugh out loud in such a sedate and quiet gathering as this.

"Do you not agree, Mr. Hughes?" Lillian addressed her question to *him* without the slightest context.

He looked to her, confused. The expectation in her expression told him quite clearly that she was attempting to draw him into her conversation and felt quite certain of her success despite his currently being engaged in a conversation with her sister.

"Agree with what, precisely, Miss Napper?"

She gave him the same coy smile she had again and again. "You never do listen, do you?"

"On the contrary, I am generally considered a good listener."

Ellie leaned forward, joining the discussion. "I have found you to be precisely that, Mr. Hughes."

Lillian shot her sister a look that sent the younger lady scooting back and abandoning the conversation.

"We were saying that at-home hours are not always enjoyable for those of us in the younger set," Lillian said. "Civility, of course, requires us to behave and not make our displeasure apparent, but I am certain each of us would far rather promenade on the Gravel Walk at the moment than sit here pretending to not be utterly bored."

"I cannot argue with that," Newton said.

"I have an excellent idea." Lillian looked from Newton to Charlie and back again several times. "We should promenade. I am certain my mother will not object, and it would be a lovely way to pass the afternoon. The weather is fine, and I am certain many of our friends will be out doing precisely that."

Newton looked to Ellie, intending to defer to her. Lillian, however, jumped ahead.

"Mother," she said, interrupting, apparently without concern, the conversation occurring just beyond their little circle. "These kind gentlemen have invited us to promenade along the Gravel Walk with them. May we, please?"

That was not at all an accurate recounting of things.

Charlie quickly salvaged the situation. "It is the hour when most people meander. We would be honored to accompany your daughters, if that is what they wish."

Perfectly managed, that. He'd offered no insult and no direct contradiction while still making it clear that they had not, in fact, proposed the idea and nor were they the ones who fancied the arrangement. Brilliant. Newton wished he had even half Charlie Jonquil's social prowess.

"As we would not wish to cast any aspersions on your daughters' characters," Charlie continued, "I would request that a maid be provided."

Lillian objected, leaning a bit toward Newton as she did. "I am certain that is not necessary. You are gentlemen in every sense, and I feel quite safe with both of you."

"We insist," Newton said.

For just a moment, Lillian seemed speechless. She finally settled on, "How considerate."

Through it all, Ellie didn't say a word. The moment her sister had interrupted, she'd grown quiet. Once her mother had been pulled into the discussion, Ellie's eyes had dropped to her clasped hands, a shrinking posture not unlike her display at the first ball they'd both attended.

"Allow us a moment to fetch our wraps," Lillian said.

Apparently, the excursion was moving forward despite Mrs. Napper's not having actually given her approval. Ellie, Newton, and Charlie were meant to participate, but not one of them had shown any enthusiasm. Lillian was not one to be distracted from her purpose.

"Ellie." Lillian pushed her sister's whispered name through clenched teeth. "We need to fetch our wraps."

"Oh, am I invited on your promenade?" Though she asked the question demurely, there was a hint of cheek in the question.

"Elfrida." Mrs. Napper's tone was not the least subtle or gentle.

Even that tiny hint of fire Ellie had shown when addressing her sister disappeared. She rose, eyes still a bit lowered, and slipped from the room.

Newton and Charlie offered their hostess a quick farewell, indicating they would bring the sisters home after the outing.

They made their way to the front vestibule to wait for the young ladies' return and stood in pointedly awkward silence. Charlie never had objected to Newton's preference for quiet. The discomfort in that moment grew, rather, out of displeasure over the task forced upon them and, at least on Newton's part, irritation with Mrs. Napper's treatment of Ellie.

The sisters returned quickly, their wool wraps around their shoulders and bonnets atop their heads.

"One of the maids has received leave from the housekeeper to accompany us." Lillian made the declaration with the authority of the mistress of the house rather than the daughter of the estate. One could not argue against her sense of confidence.

"Her name is Molly," Ellie said. "She has a reliable sense of propriety but isn't overly meddling. She'll be just perfect."

"Ellie, you mustn't bore the gentlemen with details about the servants, for heaven's sake."

A war played out in Ellie's expression. She clearly wished to rise to her own defense but was reluctant to do so.

"For my part, Miss Ellie," Newton said, "I have never been bored by any conversation I have had with you."

Her smile blossomed into a look of gratitude. "What a kind thing to say."

"I am sincere. You are excellent company." Newton offered her his arm as they moved toward the door. He was not merely playing a role; he genuinely looked forward to spending the length of the promenade with her.

Lillian eyed him as he passed with her sister. The lady was clearly not pleased. Charlie motioned her through the door. Manners would require him to, at some point, make the expected offering of his arm, but his slight delay would make certain Lillian didn't simply switch targets.

By the time they reached the Gravel Walk, Charlie had maneuvered a four-wide arrangement, with Ellie between the two of them and Lillian on his other side. With a degree of acumen that was almost shocking, Charlie managed to pay equal attention to both sisters without giving even the tiniest hint of a preference. Newton was far enough removed from Lillian to prevent conversation, which was preferable.

"Miss Lancaster has insisted that I am to be numbered amongst the Huntresses when they descend upon London for the Season." Ellie grinned up at him. Utter joyfulness emanated from her. "I know you have spent a little time in Town for the social whirl. Are the Huntresses as mischievous in London as they have proven in Bath?"

"More so," Newton said. "They turn heads, I will say that. And there are three you have not yet met."

"Truly?" Eagerness grew in her expression. "Three more." She blinked and shook her head. "But they aren't actually scandalous?"

It was not a simple question to answer. "They earn a few tsks and raised eyebrows here and there, but none of them causes too much consternation. They are mostly viewed as amusingly unique."

"They sound delightful," Ellie said.

"They sound like trouble." Lillian had, apparently, overheard.

"Like I said," Ellie muttered under her breath.

Newton held back a laugh but only just.

"You should smile more often, Mr. Hughes," Ellie said. "You are quite handsome when you do."

"Ellie, do have some decorum." Lillian sounded entirely horrified. "A lady simply does not say such things to a gentleman."

"Decorum requires me to lie?"

Through tight lips, Lillian countered, "Decorum requires you to behave."

Newton lowered his head a bit and his voice a lot. "Please don't. I enjoy when you make a bit merry."

She beamed once more. "No one has ever said that to me before."

They kept their conversation quiet so as not to be overheard by Lillian.

"I'd wager our friend Miss Lancaster would agree that you are an enjoyable companion."

Ellie took a deep breath, releasing it slowly. "I do hope I am able to join her in London. I'm not certain my parents will allow it. I am the youngest, after all."

"If you are able to be in Town for the Season, I hope you will allow me to call on you and request that you stand up with me at any balls we might both attend. I would enjoy being granted your company again."

She set her free hand on his arm, looking up at him with such a kind and pleased expression. "I do believe that is the most words I have heard from you at one time."

"And far more than you spoke whilst at home with your mother."

Her shoulders drooped a bit. "She is easier to endure if I play the role she prefers."

"You play a great many roles, Ellie," he said. "Do you ever grow weary of them?"

She nodded. He nodded.

They were both playing parts, after all. Perhaps the Bard had been correct. All the world was but a stage and all the men and women merely players.

The question remained, Was *this* act fated to be a comedy or a tragedy?

CHAPTER EIGHT

ELLIE HAD BEEN UNCERTAIN WHEN Artemis had first suggested that Newton be her partner in the madcap scheme the two of them had cooked up over tea at the Pump Room. Her friend had insisted he would not only be willing but would also be an enjoyable partner in crime. He was so quiet and withdrawn, and his assessing expression was more than a little intimidating. He had seemed such a peculiar choice.

Ellie had seldom been so pleased to be wrong about another person.

As she waited in the vestibule for her parents to descend the stairs and announce the family ready to trek to that week's Fancy Ball, excitement bubbled inside. Newton would be there; he had told her so. She could hardly wait to see him and talk with him again.

"I do hope you mean to behave today," Lillian said, standing nearby. She didn't look at Ellie, but there was no doubt to whom the comment was directed. They, alone, stood there.

"Of course." Ellie had heard her mother utter that phrase so many times that it emerged from her own lips almost without thought.

"Do not act as though I haven't reason for concern." Still, she didn't look at Ellie. "You monopolized Mr. Hughes's time during our promenade. You were bolder than you ought to have been, and it was not the first time. At the Lancaster home, you turned a simple evening of short answers into a battle of wits."

"Which I won, you will recall."

"Gentlemen do not wish to connect themselves to overly forward ladies. Or their families."

Ellie had heard this argument before. For once, she did not shrug and keep her peace. "I do not wish to connect myself to any gentleman who insists I pretend to be bacon-brained so he can feel reassured of his own intelligence."

"You are going to be the ruin of this family, Elfrida. Mark my words."

Lillian only ever used Ellie's full name when she was truly upset with her. Ellie would do well to tread lightly that evening.

Mother and Father joined them a moment later, dressed in their finest and appearing both nervous and excited. They had a claim on Society, at least in Bath. But that claim was minor compared to most. The one time her parents had gone to London, hoping to secure an advantageous match for Ellie's oldest sister, they had discovered just how comparatively low their rung on the ladder really was.

Ellie loved hearing Artemis and Daria and Gillian talk about their adventures in Town. She longed to join them, longed to claim the invitation Artemis had already extended. But the chances of her parents taking her there were nonexistent.

"We had best be on our way," Father said.

"Of course," Mother answered.

They were soon settled in the carriage. Ellie kept her excitement hidden. She could hold back her thoughts and feelings and the things she wanted to say until she saw Newton. He would be happy to hear her and see her. He wouldn't tell her to behave or tuck herself behind an ill-fitting role. He wouldn't look at her with the disapproval that her own family did. She was looking forward to his company.

Her eyes scanned the expansive ballroom the moment they stepped inside. Finding a particular person in the swirling crowd would be difficult. She hoped luck would prove kind. It did.

"I see Miss Lancaster," Ellie said. "I mean to go bid her good evening."

"Do allow her to come to you," Mother whispered anxiously. "You will appear overly bold if you approach someone of her standing."

"We are known to be friends, Mother. No one will think anything untoward in my approaching her."

"Spending time with her has made you forget yourself." Father didn't often speak scoldingly. He did then. "She is sister-in-law and ward to the Duke of Kielder. Her siblings include a duchess and a countess. Her brother is married to an exceptionally close family friend of the Earl of Lampton. Though Miss Lancaster has shown you kindness, no doubt owing to our having once been neighbors, you are not her equal. To pretend otherwise is the height of folly."

She wanted to insist he was wrong. But he wasn't entirely. She wasn't Artemis's equal, but that didn't mean she would be unwelcome. Difficult experience had taught her not to argue with her parents on these matters. She behaved in the ways they insisted she behave. She kept her peace when she wanted nothing more than to defend herself.

She remained at her parents' side, waiting for her friend to see her and come over. She hated the thought of needing to be rescued. Lillian might've been content to play the part of the helpless damsel incapable of doing anything for herself, but that was Ellie's idea of absolute torture. They slowly made a circuit of the ballroom, Mother and Father greeting people they knew, addressing with great deference those they wished they knew better. All the while, Ellie watched Artemis and Daria, who had now found each other. At one point, she caught a glimpse of Gillian but was not able to catch her eye either. What a misery this would be if she spent the entire evening silently crushed by the weight of her family's disapproval, watching from a distance as her newfound friends enjoyed the freedom she was not afforded. If only they could simply go to London now.

As she and her parents began their second turn about the room, a voice broke into the silence enveloping Ellie.

"A pleasure to see you again, Mr. Napper, Mrs. Napper." That the greeting came from Newton himself was a most welcome and wonderful surprise. Ellie looked over at him just as he looked to her. Manners dictated that he greet her older sister first, which he did, employing a pleasant but impersonal tone. Then, with the tiniest hint of a smile, he gave Ellie his full attention. "Miss Ellie. I had hoped you would be here this evening."

"Lillian was hoping *you* would be here." One would never accuse Mother of being a master in the art of subtlety.

"I do not wish to be overly hasty," Newton said. "But I am certain Miss Ellie's dances are nearly all claimed. I wish to secure my turn to stand up with her for a set, if she has one remaining." Then, being the gentleman he was, he looked to Lillian. "And you too, of course."

Mother appeared confused for the length of a breath. "Of course. Of course they will dance with you. You simply must begin with Lillian. She is quite an adept dancer."

Newton hesitated for only the briefest moment. It was enough, Ellie hoped, to at least make her parents wonder if his attachment to Lillian was forming as quickly and fully as they wanted to believe. That was, after all, the point of their efforts.

Lillian accepted Newton's invitation for the very next set. The bubble of jealousy that expanded around Ellie's heart caught her unawares. She wasn't consumed by it, and she didn't intend to sulk. But she was a little sad. She'd missed him and had been looking forward to his company. As too often happened, Lillian stood between her and happiness.

"The Hugheses are a fine family," Father said. "An association with them is quite a fine thing. For Ellie to have gained something of a friendship with Miss Lancaster and Mr. Jonquil, as well as the Mullins siblings and Miss Phelps, is quite a feather in our cap. And for Mr. Hughes to continually return to spend time with our daughters is encouraging."

Our daughters. That was not at all the view of it Ellie wanted her parents to have. But at least they were not interpreting Newton's presence as particular interest in Lillian.

"You did not tell me how things transpired while you were promenading yesterday." Mother looked to Ellie with concern and anticipation in her gaze.

"I had assumed Lillian would give you a full report." Indeed, it seemed odd that she hadn't.

"She was quiet after returning. That has me concerned that things did not go well with her efforts in Mr. Newton's direction."

That was truer than Mother likely realized. Ellie, however, was not going to admit as much. She was scolded for being overly forward and speaking too much, but the repercussions of admitting that she was personally undermining her sister's chances would likely instigate a punishment more severe than she had yet experienced. "Mr. Newton seemed in good spirits throughout. He asked questions of both of us: where we had traveled, what our home was like, what our future plans were."

Mother looked at her father with an expression of concern.

"He asked about our estate?" Father didn't sound pleased with the topic of conversation.

"Among other things."

Mother and Father looked at each other, wearing nearly identical expressions of dismay.

"Forgive my confusion," Ellie said, "but I am not certain why that is of such concern." Discussions of homes and estates were common among *tonish* people.

"Our estate, our home, our situation are lowly compared to the Hugheses'. We can claim nothing that comes close to what they can. Their family holdings outshine ours in every conceivable way."

Mother twisted her hands around each other, her eyes darting about the way they did when she was thinking frantically. "Did he seem dismissive . . . or disgusted?"

Ellie shook her head. "He gave no indication of disapproval." And yet, she found herself wondering.

He was paying her attention as both a favor to her, which he likely did out of a sense of gentlemanly kindness, and as a means of being instrumental in his own matrimonial escape. That did not mean he approved of her or looked upon her circumstances with anything but a kind and quiet indifference. Surely, she had not misread him so entirely. She did not think he was a talented actor. Indeed, he was so circumspect and withdrawn that he was far more likely to make an awkward mull of any pretended feelings. Then again, he was doing precisely that and at her bidding.

She didn't entirely know what to believe. That was, she supposed, the danger one courted when undertaking a ruse such as this. How easy it would be to allow herself to believe things that were not true simply because it was easier to do so.

Was it all an act? Perhaps her forwardness caused him consternation that he simply kept hidden. Perhaps he did not object to enacting the charade for his own sake but actually found her humble circumstances a bit lowering.

No. She did not believe that. There was too much sincerity in him. They were pretending that tenderness was growing between them, but his kindness to her was not a ruse. She felt confident she could think of him as a friend.

In the midst of her mental wanderings, her path finally crossed with Artemis's.

"At last we've found each other," Artemis said. "I saw you a few times but never could seem to reach you before you moved along. Why did you not come and greet me?"

"My parents feared that would be overly forward of me," she said. Mother and Father were listening quite intently. She would let them hear the answer to their earlier objections.

"Overly forward?" Artemis repeated the words on something of a laugh. "We are dear friends, Ellie. There is nothing overly forward about greetings between friends."

A little bubble of pride expanded in her chest. She had not been wrong about Artemis's friendship. She did not think she was wrong about Newton's either. A person needed such boosts of confidence now and then.

Artemis remained for a few minutes, talking amiably with her. Mother and Father stood in near-silent awe, a blessing by anyone's estimation. The respite was more than welcome.

By the time Artemis was pulled away by a Society acquaintance, Ellie had her doubts entirely sorted and herself firmly in hand. She was once more committed to saving herself from an unwanted match with Charlie, Lillian from forcing an unwelcome match on Newton, and Newton from being pushed into pursuing Artemis.

The set came to its conclusion, and Newton returned with Lillian. He thanked her, as was customary, then bowed to her parents.

Having undertaken the usual niceties, Newton turned to Ellie. "Your dances have not all been claimed while I was gone, have they?" He was either very good at this ruse, or he did, in fact, have some fondness for her.

"I have not been asked for a single set. Neither have I seen any indication that there's any interest beyond your offer earlier." She allowed a mischievous smile. "Are you certain you still wish to dance with me? You might be seen as having incredibly poor taste."

Though Newton smiled, her parents most certainly did not. They would far rather have preferred she be more like Lillian, whom Ellie wasn't sure was capable of independent thought. Lillian kept that part of herself locked away so firmly that even family was not privy to it.

Ellie could not live her life that way. She knew she couldn't. Newton bowed once more. "I am quite certain I still wish to dance with you. If you are permitted." He turned to her parents for the permission she was required to obtain. They both nodded but with some degree of reluctance. She felt certain it was their confusion over the difference in Newton's manner of asking her compared to the way in which he had invited Lillian. He was doing a fine job of showing that he was not inclined toward Lillian at all.

Ellie set her hand in the crook of his arm, and he led her out for the set. It was a country dance she was quite familiar with. The movements would bring them together many times. She would have an opportunity to chat with him and enjoy his company for the length of the dance.

The first time they were brought together, he asked, "Is something the matter? You seem pensive."

"I'm afraid I have endured something of a scolding."

"I'm sorry to hear that. From your sister or your parents?" He seemed genuinely compassionate.

"Both, truth be told. Lillian concluded hers before we left home. My parents continued on the same topic at our arrival."

They were separated for a time as the dance continued. His expression was unreadable. He did not seem unhappy or disapproving, but neither did he appear curious or interested. She had found, though, his expression was often neutral. When they came back together once more, he spoke first. "On what topic did they scold you? I've been trying to think of a reason for them to be disapproving, and I can think of nothing."

She smiled unabashedly. "I am afraid my family can think of ample reason for lecturing me. I know how young ladies are meant to behave, and I too often do not."

His gaze narrowed on her a little. "We are about to be separated once more. When I return to your side, I intend to quite thoroughly interrogate you on the topic of your mysterious breaches of etiquette."

She might've been intimidated if she hadn't seen mischief twinkling in his eyes. And further, she was touched that he could not immediately think of at least a half dozen breaches of etiquette, as he called them, that she had committed just during the time they had spent together. He was enough in Society to realize ladies were meant to be demure, and she was never that when not forced into decorum by her parents. He was a kind soul, Newton Hughes. How she enjoyed talking with him. His company was reassuring and soothing and kind.

His romantic interest in her was feigned. But his goodness was genuine.

As promised, he dove in when they were next together. "Have you taken up a career on the stage?"

She smiled and shook her head.

"Begun frequenting gambling dens?"

Again, she could not keep back a smile.

"Then I will assume you have gone about singing inappropriately bawdy tunes at the top of your voice in Hyde Park during the fashionable hour. There can be no other possibility."

She laughed. The sound drew a bit of attention from those nearest them. "I don't imagine it's possible for me to have done anything in Hyde Park when one takes into consideration the fact that I have not once in all my life been to London."

She was watched a little closely by those in the set dancing nearest them. Whether the confusion or curiosity or disapproval or whatever it was that she saw in their faces arose from her admission that she'd never been to Town or the fact that she had done the unthinkable and laughed whilst dancing a country set, she couldn't say. At the moment, she did not particularly care. Newton was working his magic once more, weaving a spell of contentment over her.

"Well then," he said, "I haven't the first idea what shocking infringement you are guilty of."

Ellie answered quickly before the dance pulled them apart. "I speak my mind too freely and do not pretend to be an idiot."

Though he did not breach protocol and laugh, she could see how tempted he was to do precisely that. Her heart soared. Her spirits lifted. If only this were not a pretended courtship. She was beginning to suspect that Newton Hughes was precisely the sort of gentleman with whom she could build a happy life.

But he was entirely out of reach.

CHAPTER NINE

"Laughing out loud in the midst of a dance. I've never been so humiliated in all my life." Lillian had been blustering ever since they'd returned home from the Upper Assembly Rooms the night before. "And she showed not the least embarrassment over it. I could have endured the stares had she at least appeared to recognize the impropriety of her behavior. How are we to obtain advantageous connections if she makes us the laughingstock of Society?" That seemed a bit harsh. But it fit well with most of what Lillian had been saying to and about her the last few days.

Ellie loved her sister; she truly did. But Lillian's single-minded pursuit of an auspicious match was making her more and more difficult to live with.

"I did not laugh as an intentional violation of propriety," Ellie said. "My laughter caught me off guard, I assure you. Mr. Hughes said something quite diverting, and I couldn't help myself."

Mother was not appeased by the explanation. "A lady with manners can always help herself."

"I am trying." She suspected they would not believe her, but she had to at least attempt to defend herself. If only they knew how much she did keep back, how many things she didn't say that would upset them. She was not an uncouth person. She didn't do anything truly shocking, and even her minor missteps were unintentional. They simply had expectations that required her to be someone other than the person she actually was. Did they have any idea how exhausting that was?

"I do not believe too much damage was done," Father said. "Mr. Hughes did return and speak with us again that evening. Miss Lancaster returned again and again. Mr. Jonquil was also relatively solicitous. He is showing only the most impersonal interest in Ellie, though I cannot say I blame him."

Ellie bit back a response. Her father was again joining in the backhanded comments.

"We might do best to abandon our ambitions where Mr. Jonquil is concerned." Father tapped his chin with his fingers as he thought.

Ellie inwardly sighed. They had managed one of their two goals. Charlie needn't worry any longer about her family's machinations. If only she could find a means of extricating Newton from Lillian's increasingly talon-like grip.

"Our only hope on that score," Lillian said with clear bitterness in her voice, "is to rid ourselves of Ellie. Perhaps even send her home to Shropshire. Mr. Hughes spends more time speaking with her than he ought. And whenever they are in company, she never fails to do something to embarrass our family."

"I have heard all the finest families make a regular practice of 'ridding themselves' of their children," Ellie said sarcastically. "Very refined of us."

Lillian shot her a look of frustrated disapproval.

It was Mother, however, who spoke. "You have been the cause of enough difficulties, Elfrida. Do not add impertinence to your list of infractions."

When her family was put out with her, Ellie found it best to escape. Were she at home, she would simply go for a walk about the grounds or in the gardens. She hadn't that luxury in Bath. Still, she knew how to make herself scarce.

"Perhaps, Mother, you would feel it best if I go search up the ribbon you've been suggesting I get to retrim my bonnet. I would be out of your hair for a time, and you can discuss these important matters without me making them difficult."

"Take Molly with you," Mother said. "A young lady wandering about on her own would cause even more whispers than we are already enduring."

Ellie nodded her agreement before taking her leave.

Molly was always eager for any opportunity to be out of the house. Ellie couldn't help thinking the chambermaid would have been happier at the country estate, where she would have far more opportunities for out of doors.

Ellie had something in common with the soft-spoken maid, though different lives and experiences made it difficult to have a deep or personal conversation. They were limited to comments on the weather and observations about the fashions they saw around them.

They reached the ribbon and trims shop. To Ellie's great surprise, Artemis and the Huntresses were inside, perusing ribbons and laughing amongst themselves.

Daria spotted her first. "Ellie." She rushed over, followed quickly by Artemis and more sedately by Gillian. "We are well met."

"We are, indeed," Ellie said. "Have you only just begun your shopping, or are you nearly done?"

"This was our final stop," Artemis said.

"It is my *only* stop."

"Do join us," Artemis said. "We'll see you home again. And with all of us here, you won't need a maid accompanying you."

Ellie looked to Molly. "You needn't stay. When you return to the house, do kindly tell my parents that I've joined Miss Lancaster, Miss Mullins, and Miss Phelps?"

The maid dipped a curtsy of acknowledgment. There was no missing the disappointment in her expression. Her escape hadn't been long-lived.

"If you'd care to make your way back *slowly*," Ellie said conspiratorially, "I think that would be more than reasonable."

A bit of a smile touched her face. "Yes, Miss Ellie." She left the shop with a renewed bounce in her step.

"I have often wondered how desperate the servants in our homes are to have time away from us," Gillian said.

"I am often desperate to get away from my family," Daria said with a light laugh. "I cannot imagine our servants feel any differently."

"I have a confession," Ellie said. "I am here strictly because I was desperate for some time away from *my* family."

She received words of support and empathy. What a difference it would have made to have had friends such as these during her difficult growing-up years. She might not have spent so much time hiding and pretending and wondering if she would ever get to be the person she was.

Artemis ran her fingers over a length of ribbon hanging from a rack above their heads. She lowered her voice. "Are they being unkind to you, Ellie?"

"A little. They have given up on Charlie developing a *tendre* for me. That is a positive development. But they are upset that Newton isn't showing more interest in Lillian."

Artemis nodded. "Lillian is likely equally unhappy about that?"

"She is."

"Are they blaming you?"

Ellie sighed. "Yes. My 'untoward' behavior is driving him away, they say. I've embarrassed them and him and am ruining absolutely everything."

Artemis eyed her a bit narrowly. "They aren't upset at the possibility that you are . . . *stealing* him away from your sister?"

She snorted. "I don't think they consider me capable of turning any gentleman's head, especially if Lillian hasn't managed it."

"For what it is worth," Artemis said, "I believe you have turned Newton's head a little. He likes your company; I can see that he does."

"Truly?"

"I cannot say precisely the leaning of his regard, but he does like spending time with you, no matter your family's skepticism."

Ellie took comfort in that. Artemis was an expert in being whoever and whatever a situation demanded. She was the epitome of sweetness at certain matrons' at-homes, then something of a harmless flirt when participating in parlor games with gentlemen their age, then a bit of a dragon when determined to get her way. Yet Ellie had no reason not to believe her in this moment. Artemis had ever been honest with her, even when that honesty had been wrapped in dramatics.

"I wish I could be hopeful that my family would take me to London when the Season arrives next year," Ellie said. "But I am quite certain they won't. They might take Lillian, but even that seems unlikely."

Artemis motioned to the shopkeeper that she was interested in a length of the deep-green ribbon hanging near Ellie. He dipped his head and moved to the wall full of drawers, where his goods were kept.

"You have told your parents that I expressed a desire for you to be in London?" Artemis returned to the topic at hand.

"I did."

Artemis shook her head. "With how much store they put by status and wealth, that ought to have convinced them to jump at the opportunity. As tiring as it is to be pretentious, it is useful at times. My brother-in-law taught me that." Her terrifying, dictatorial brother-in-law, no doubt.

"I am certain they would have seized the chance for such an important connection, but my mother did not believe me when I told her of it."

A look of deepening understanding entered Artemis's expression.

"You aren't coming to London, Ellie?" Gillian looked thoroughly disappointed. "You have to. The Huntresses won't be complete without you. And you haven't even met the others yet."

She'd known these ladies less than a fortnight, and they already considered her a crucial part of their group. She couldn't possibly give that up and return to being the scolded and dismissed youngest daughter on an isolated estate in an isolated corner of the kingdom.

"We will think of something," Artemis said. "The Huntresses are not easily defeated."

"We are, however, easily soaked." Daria motioned to the front windows.

The skies had burst open. Rain pelted the glass, falling hard on the scrambling passersby.

"Heavens," Gillian said. "I did not even think to bring an umbrella."

"Perhaps it will not last long." Ellie watched the downpour, her heart dropping. Had Molly managed to reach home or duck into a shop somewhere?

If the rain lasted too long, she herself would have to brave it. Mother would be none too pleased if she ruined her dress. Their sojourn in Bath had not been without expense, and her parents were put out enough already without her adding to their displeasure.

The bell over the shop door rang, accompanying the sound of scrambling feet. People were escaping the deluge, taking refuge where they could find it.

"A ribbon shop?" A gentleman objected with a laugh. "Could you not have suggested we duck into a tobacconist's or a bootmaker's?"

Ellie felt certain she knew the voice. She looked to her companions, curious if they, too, found the voice familiar. One glance at Artemis sorted the mystery. She had a particular expression of ruffled feathers and prim propriety reserved exclusively for this one person: Charlie Jonquil.

"If your sense of manhood cannot survive a momentary sojourn in a ribbon shop, then you have more significant troubles than this rainfall." That, Ellie knew immediately, was Newton. He spoke more with Charlie than anyone else and showed himself quite clever and funny, though he had begun to open up with her as well.

That Charlie immediately laughed spoke well of *his* sense of humor. Ellie was grateful to have come to know both gentlemen better.

The two came around a corner and spotted the Huntresses standing near the window. All exchanged bows and curtsies. Charlie's smile set Daria and Gillian a little aflutter but without any of the silliness too many young ladies employed. They found him handsome but refused to be ridiculous.

"I see the lot of you managed to be indoors when the heavens burst into tears," Charlie said.

"What do you suppose they're crying about?" Artemis asked a touch too innocently. "Something you ought not to have done?"

"Not I," Charlie said. "I've been a saint."

Artemis's mouth twisted tightly to one side. She returned her gaze to the rain-pelted window.

"Have you been a saint as well, Mr. Hughes?" Ellie felt a bit odd addressing him so formally, but she didn't dare make use of his Christian name in public.

"Always."

Charlie shook his head in obvious amusement. "Fortunately for you, my friend, we aren't terribly near a church. You'd be struck by lightning on the instant."

"Only if I were standing too close to *you*."

Their banter marked a long and friendly association. Ellie would have loved to have a friendship like that. She felt the beginnings of it with Artemis and the Huntresses. If she could only get to London, their friendship would grow and deepen. If only.

"The skies are quite leaden," Artemis said. "We might be prisoners here for hours and hours."

Charlie pulled in a tense breath through flared nostrils. He crossed to her and gave her an umbrella.

She eyed it, confused. "You wish to be rid of me?"

"My father's hair had a good bit of curl in it. I don't remember much about him, but I do recall what a mess it became in the rain." Charlie eyed Artemis's curls. "Yours would be a disaster."

Ellie fully expected Artemis to scoff or ruffle up. She didn't. "Rain is my greatest nemesis."

A hint of a smile tugged at his lips. "I thought *I* was your greatest nemesis."

"You have your moments."

With a silent laugh, Charlie turned back toward Newton. The two exchanged looks of laughing weariness.

"Have you umbrellas for all of us?" Ellie asked. "You will find yourself the greatest nemesis of three additional people otherwise."

Charlie appeared both diverted and repentant. "Newton has one. But I am afraid, between us, we have only the two."

Newton looked over the group, thinking. "Two of you could share an umbrella; that would allow all four of you to escape drier than you would otherwise."

"What of you and Charlie?" Ellie didn't care for the idea of either of them being left a cold, sodden mess.

"We, it seems, are the ones who will be prisoners in this ribbon shop."

Charlie leaned a shoulder against the nearby wall, arms folded casually across his chest. "Rather inconsiderate of your parents to live so far from this establishment, Newton. They ought to have thought that through better."

Newton nodded solemnly.

Daria chimed in. "Artemis's brother lives near here. I'd wager we could hurry there without being entirely drenched if we put our minds to it."

They all looked to Artemis. Would she object to the idea of offering Charlie refuge?

"I daresay my brother would be pleased to see the gentlemen." Artemis shrugged. "He is inexplicably fond of Charlie."

"Excellent." Daria slipped up beside Artemis. "Shall we?"

Newton held his umbrella out to Ellie.

"But you will be soaked through," she said.

He smiled gently. "I won't be felled by a bit of rain."

"This is far more than 'a bit.'"

He held the umbrella closer still, indicating he fully intended for her to take it.

She hesitated.

"I do not shrivel in the rain, Miss Ellie. But I would be horrified to see you pelted by the downpour. I would not wish to see you miserable."

Kind and thoughtful, as always. "Thank you."

Artemis was given her length of green ribbon. She thanked the shopkeeper, then motioned for them all to be on their way.

The four ladies, protected by the two umbrellas, and the two gentlemen, far less protected by the brims of their tall hats, rushed from the shop and into the rain. The cloudburst had lightened a little from what it had been. They were still getting wet but not as much as they would have mere minutes earlier, though the journey to the Lancasters' home was long enough to see their gowns caked in the muck and dirt of the city and dripping with rain. The gentlemen were in even worse shape.

They were let into the house by a confused and overwhelmed Henson. He didn't seem to have the least idea what to do.

Artemis, as was usual for her, took immediate charge of the situation. "Henson, do show the gentlemen to the guest bedchamber, and ask Mr. Lancaster if he can provide them with a change of clothing." She eyed Charlie. "You are taller than he is, so I cannot speak to the fit of anything he has to offer."

"At this point, I am not particular." Indeed, the poor gentleman was shivering. They both were.

"Huntresses"—Artemis motioned them onward—"follow me, and I will see all of you warm and changed into dry clothes in no time."

Borrowing clothes from Artemis? Ellie was several inches shorter than her friend and several inches more . . . expansive, as it were. If Artemis could find a single thing in her wardrobe that fit Ellie, she would be more than justified in claiming "worker of miracles" amongst her accomplishments.

For Ellie's part, she resigned herself to being relegated to a private bed-chamber to dry off in a blanket, wishing she'd simply stayed home.

CHAPTER TEN

NEITHER NEWTON NOR CHARLIE WAS built much like Mr. Lancaster. Charlie was taller and more slender. Newton was a touch shorter than either of them and not nearly as broad shouldered as their host. The former lieutenant's clothes—his blessedly dry clothes—were an odd fit on both of them. Yet, they were both remarkably grateful to no longer be dripping and shivering with cold.

Mrs. Lancaster invited all of her soggy guests to the sitting room once they were dry. Upon entering, Newton and Charlie found themselves the recipients of hot tea and hot soup. A low fire was burning, and heavy throws were passed around to provide added warmth and comfort.

Charlie had spoken often about Mr. and Mrs. Lancaster. He'd spoken in such glowing terms, Newton hadn't truly believed it was possible for the actual people behind the praise to live up to his description. If anything, Charlie had not been effusive enough.

The young ladies had not yet joined them. There were more of them, after all, and, at least to his minute understanding of such things, had more complicated clothing. It likely would take them a while. So he and Charlie sat quietly, waiting. It was a warm and comfortable arrangement.

After a time, Mr. and Mrs. Lancaster joined them as well.

"Thank you for your generous hospitality," Newton said. "We descended upon you without warning."

Mr. Lancaster waved that off. "I'm pleased you thought to come here. Being caught in a downpour such as we have just had would be miserable even for the hardiest of people. Being a former navy man myself, I know what it is to be soaked to the bones. I'm grateful you did not have to endure that for long."

"You are always welcome here," Mrs. Lancaster said.

One often encountered marriages in which the wife was quite silent and the husband spoke on behalf of them both. Far too often the arrangement appeared to be a forced one. That was not the case here. Mrs. Lancaster gave the clear impression of preferring to be quiet and even seemed grateful when her husband filled in the gaps. Whether she was simply shy amongst people she didn't know well or shy in general, he could not yet say. Whatever the case might be, he found no reason to be worried for her.

He did, however, worry for Ellie. He only wished he were in a position to do something to relieve that misery she experienced at home.

"The rain does appear to have a let up a little," Charlie said. "Word likely ought to be sent to the young ladies' homes while there is a slight break in the weather so their families don't worry about their whereabouts." It was a thoughtful gesture, one quite common to Charlie. Truth be told, all the Jonquils were known for their thoughtfulness, even Charlie's oldest brother, who was also known to be something of an eccentric. Artemis often berated Charlie, but he was a good sort.

Mrs. Lancaster broke her usual silence once more. "We did send word around. The girls' families will be happy to know they are safe and warm and dry."

That settled everyone's worries. A moment later, the warm, dry ladies themselves arrived among them, chattering and talking with the enthusiasm of young ladies taking a brisk and invigorating walk in the country rather than having only just ducked out of a monumental downpour. Their spirits were not flagged by their earlier misery.

Despite himself, Newton found his eye following Ellie in particular. She was such a joy to spend time with, clever and amiable, thoughtful and intelligent. She had become a particularly good friend.

The new arrivals were soon seated, allowing the gentlemen to sit again, and provided with the same warming refreshments that he and Charlie had already indulged in. Artemis sat as far from Charlie as could possibly be managed without actually leaving the room or the group of friends. Newton suspected she was not usually so begrudging in her friendships and welcomes. It was remarkably intriguing.

To Newton's delight, Ellie sat near him. Everyone in this group knew their courtship was not real. She didn't have to continue with the charade here. Had she forgotten that? Or was she sitting beside him because she genuinely wished to? And, perhaps more to the point, which answer did he most wish were true?

The gowns Ellie usually wore were not anywhere near the first stare of fashion. She never looked dowdy nor truly unpresentable. He thought her quite pretty, truth be told.

The dress she now donned, which she had apparently borrowed from Artemis, was extremely fashionable. It was a shade of deep purple that somehow made her brown eyes almost golden. And it brought out a hue of honey in her hair he had not noticed before. She was not built on an identical scale with Artemis. To that, their proportions were not at all the same. Yet the dress fit her well.

Indeed, all the young ladies' borrowed gowns looked as though they were made for the wearer. Either Artemis's lady's maid had been remarkably hard at work pinning and taping the various gowns to fit their temporary wearers, or they'd somehow procured gowns elsewhere. Whatever the case might be, Newton found himself unable to look away. He didn't consider himself a shallow gentleman. He did not place physical appearance above all else. But there was something different in Ellie just now, beyond her more fashionable and striking appearance. She glowed with apparent happiness. Dressing in a fine gown and looking to advantage seemed to have inspired a change in how she viewed herself. There was a confidence there that rang truer than her usual air of self-assurance.

"You look very lovely," he said. Only after he offered the compliment did he realize it might not have been entirely appropriate. They were not actually courting, after all.

But Ellie, true to form, accepted the compliment with a breezy and pleased demeanor. "Thank you. It really is beautiful. And it fits me so well. I don't know how Artemis managed to find anything amongst her gowns that would fit me when my proportions are so different from her own."

"Artemis?" he pressed. "Was she directly involved in acquiring your dress?"

She grinned unrepentantly. "Artemis threw open the doors of her wardrobe and pulled out two gowns without needing to even think it through and simultaneously sent one of the maids for a dress in her sister-in-law's wardrobe. The three were perfectly suited to the one of us she intended it for. Different colors, different styles, but exactly what looks best on each of us. And then, as nimbly and quickly as any lady's maid one could hope for—more so even— Artemis pulled out dress pins and tape and ribbons and temporarily altered each of the gowns to fit us beautifully. I'm half-convinced she's more witch than seamstress."

Newton made a sound of pondering. "Witchcraft, for sure."

Ellie sipped at her tea, her eyes dancing with merriment. "Do you suppose the infamous Duke of Kielder would go on an absolute raging rampage if he knew his sister-in-law and ward wished to be a mantua-maker?"

"Does she?" he asked.

"I don't know for certain. I suppose it doesn't matter either way. She wouldn't be permitted to pursue it. And not only because her guardian is such a fearsome gentleman but because those are the limitations of the rules set upon her. Set upon all of us, really."

Newton knew that all too well. "It is a shame people aren't permitted to pursue those things that would fulfill and appeal to them, especially when what they long for isn't truly inappropriate, nor is it hurtful to anyone."

Ellie nodded. "It isn't as though Artemis would be taking up the life of a highwayman."

"Or as if I wish to be a villainous criminal rather than a barrister."

Ellie looked at him over the top of her teacup. He hadn't meant to make that confession. What was it about her that pulled things from him that he hadn't intended to say?

"I find your parents' objections strange. Being a barrister is not considered an inappropriate profession for a gentleman. Why, Charlie has a brother who is a barrister; no one can argue the Jonquils do not abide by propriety." Her mouth pulled into a twist of thought. "His older brother is something of a dandy and perhaps a bit more outlandish than is generally seen, but I've never seen him behave in a way that was truly unbecoming of a gentleman; neither have I heard any rumors that he has."

Newton had made all the same arguments to his parents. Charlie had made these arguments to Newton. But in the end, his parents would not be swayed. "They consider it an insult that I would wish for any profession since my father's estate provides me with ample income."

"I am sorry." Ellie briefly touched her hand to his arm. "When parents get the notion that their children are meant to serve their egos and the way they are perceived in Society, the children's best interests go by the wayside. We become tokens of success rather than people they are meant to care about." It was too specific and quick an answer to not have come from any difficult experience.

"Your parents have plans for you as well, then?"

"Of course," she said in a perfect imitation of her mother. Newton couldn't help but laugh. "My parents have no sons. They have decided the purpose of their daughters is to improve their situation by marrying well. Of course, the definition of 'well' is limited to monetary gain and improvements and social standing. My older sister married a gentleman who had none of those things, but he loves her. She successfully resisted all my parents' attempts to court someone they approved of. Lillian and I will not be so fortunate."

"If you'll forgive me for saying so," Newton said, "your nearest sister does not seem intent upon avoiding that mercenary sort of match."

Ellie acknowledged his statement with an uptick of her eyebrows and the slightest upward twist of her mouth. "Yes, Lillian shares their ambitions."

"Do *you?*"

She allowed her smile to fully blossom once more. "If I did, would I be undertaking this mischievous plot with you?"

"I suppose not."

They continued talking, mostly on light topics. She was easy to talk with. And she participated in the varied conversations going on around them. Some young ladies struggled with that, thanks to the gaps in their education as a result of the dictates of a Society that valued them far too little.

Newton had never considered himself a gifted conversationalist. He often struggled to speak at length with people; he was not unlike their hostess, except he wished he weren't quite so reserved. There was something joyful about the company of someone who made being more of who he wanted to be an easier thing to accomplish.

After they had consumed their tea and were warm again, a missive arrived. It was delivered, as was expected, to Mrs. Lancaster. After quickly glancing at it, she looked up at the gathering. "It is from the Nappers."

Newton's attention immediately turned to Ellie. She had, quite to his dismay, paled and grown still.

Across the way, all could hear Mrs. Lancaster unfold the parchment, the missive creaking with stiffness. Mrs. Lancaster read in silence. After a moment, she rose and crossed to Ellie. "There was a missive included for you." She handed a letter, folded much smaller than the one she had received, to Ellie.

"I hope they were not rude to you," Ellie said.

Mrs. Lancaster shook her head no. "But you look as though you expect them to be unkind to you."

Ellie sighed almost silently. "They generally are."

Mrs. Lancaster's quiet and reassuring features folded into a look of utmost empathy. "The household I was raised in was much the same. I am sorry you have experienced that as well. No one should feel unsafe in their own home."

Newton hadn't heard Mrs. Lancaster speak so many words at one time. That she pulled herself from her place of quiet comfort to offer kindness and understanding spoke well of her. It was little wonder that the Lancaster family adored this member of their clan.

The room was silent as Ellie's eyes scanned her letter line by line. Her pallor did not abate. Two spots of high color appeared on her cheeks, deepening the further she read. Though he could not be certain, Newton thought he detected tears in her eyes. He looked over at Artemis, intending to silently plead for her to come comfort her friend. Newton would have liked to have done it himself, but he knew that even in the context of their feigned courtship, he was not permitted to do so.

Artemis did not have to be told. She hopped from her seat and crossed to Ellie, sat on the arm of her chair, and put her arm about her friend. Artemis was clearly reading over Ellie's shoulder. Ellie did not raise any objections. At one point, Artemis's eyes pulled wide and a quiet gasp escaped her lips. Whatever the Nappers had said to their daughter was, by all appearances, shocking. Based on the pain in Ellie's face, this letter held nothing good.

Ellie lowered the letter onto her lap and looked over at Mr. and Mrs. Lancaster. "I am afraid I must return home immediately."

Mr. Lancaster shook his head. "I can't permit that. The weather is still poor. You would be soaked to the bone. I would not wish you to grow ill."

"My parents specifically instructed me to not allow the weather to be used as an excuse for remaining."

"Miss Ellie," Mr. Lancaster said, "I assure you I have never been one to be bullied into being anything less than a gentleman. I will write to your parents myself and tell them you are to remain until I feel the weather is fine enough for you to venture forth. They may question my decision if they wish, but I will not be moved."

The tears fell from Ellie's eyes in earnest. They might've been tears of worry or relief or exhaustion. Whatever their source, Newton's heart broke to see them. He reached over and set his hand on hers, wrapping his fingers around hers. Hang proprieties. She was in distress, and he could not bear it.

Artemis rose to her feet with the regal bearing of her namesake goddess. "No, Linus. I mean to amend your letter. Let us, you and I, write to the Nappers and tell them our Ellie will not be returning today because I have invited her to be my particular guest. They may object to the dictates of the weather, but they would not dare to balk at me." The fierceness of her expression and fierceness of her posture would have set even the royal family quaking in that moment.

Charlie, who was usually quite annoyed at her dramatics, silently applauded. The Huntresses nodded in firm agreement, tossing in words of encouragement and support. Ellie looked to Newton.

"This is your salvation, Ellie," he said. "Seize it."

CHAPTER ELEVEN

THE NEXT TWENTY-FOUR HOURS WERE overwhelming. Ellie's belongings were brought to the Lancaster home. The note she had received the previous day had called her judgment into question, insisted her welcome would be worn to a thread within moments of her arrival, and declared she couldn't possibly know how to behave properly and, therefore, was most certainly embarrassing them all and making a fool of herself. It wasn't anything Ellie hadn't been told before, but to read those harsh words after having had such a pleasant and welcoming interval with Artemis, the Huntresses, Charlie, and, most especially, Newton had been too jarring for her equilibrium.

Then, just as she began to feel as though she had her feet under her again, Mother and Lillian called at the Lancasters' house. Ellie had no illusions that the visit was a friendly one, given their last communication. The look on Lillian's face only further convinced Ellie to brace herself for the worst.

Ellie sat on a chair across from her sister, providing Ellie an unobstructed view of Lillian's hard, unyielding pout. It wasn't petulant; it was something far closer to angry. Had they not been granted privacy for this visit, Lillian would have kept her expression far more neutral.

"This is most unusual, you know," Mother whispered, eyeing the opulent room. "I am certain people in Society are wondering why you've left home."

"I am here as the particular guest of Artemis Lancaster," Ellie said. "That is far from a comedown. Indeed, it will reflect well on our family's standing."

"I was making adequate strides in that area," Lillian insisted. "This scheme of yours is inexcusable."

"It is not a scheme. I made no suggestion that I stay here, no request that I be taken in. Artemis insisted on it without my input whatsoever."

Lillian's mouth pulled tight. "And your audacity in calling someone of Miss Lancaster's standing by her Christian name is shocking."

"She asked me to." Ellie's jaw was tightening right along with her sister's expression.

"I needn't remind you," Mother said, "that Lillian and your father and I are working diligently toward securing a match with Mr. Hughes. Do not ruin that."

"I have spent time with Mr. Hughes—he is a close friend of the Lancasters and Mr. Jonquil—and I have not seen any indication that he is interested in Lillian."

"Likely because you spend your time with him giggling instead of helping our cause," Lillian said. "It's unseemly, you know."

"As unseemly as doggedly pursuing a disinterested gentleman?" Ellie asked under her breath.

Lillian's expression somehow hardened further. "You have no understanding of the obstacles we face. Do not mock me for *not* being as ignorant as you are."

"I am not ignorant."

"Then you are a fool." Lillian looked away, her mouth set in a line of disapproval.

Mother was a bit more conciliatory. "Please, Ellie, do not make our situation worse. Yes, being Miss Lancaster's particular guest is a welcome opportunity, but only if you do not misbehave and turn it into a disaster, as you do with so many things."

She had been told often enough that she was a misbehaved embarrassment for her to know perfectly well her tendency to "turn opportunities into disasters." For once, she would have liked to have received a compliment or a vote of confidence. She would have settled for a neutral comment.

"Do not make yourself a burden on this household," Mother said. "Do not assume you are invited every time the Lancaster family attends a social event."

Ellie nodded.

"And do not insist any of their maids see to your morning preparations at the expense of their own duties. The Lancasters do not employ them on *your* behalf."

"I know."

"Do you though?" Lillian asked dryly.

Ellie and her sister had never been as close as some sisters were, but this degree of animosity was new. She looked to her mother, hoping for some support there, some insistence that Lillian be less hostile. None was forthcoming.

"Have they shown any indications of growing weary at having you here?" Mother asked.

"They have offered nothing but words of welcome and kindness," Ellie said.

"I suspect they have," Mother acknowledged. "But likely only because they are too well-mannered to allow that weariness to be obvious."

Did her mother truly think no one could possibly have her in their company for twenty-four hours without wishing to be rid of her? Her own mother found her tedious and unwaveringly *de trop*.

Mother regaled Ellie with instructions for not making herself a nuisance. And Lillian treated her to absolute silence. By the time the two of them left, Ellie was exhausted. She didn't even accompany them to the front door to bid them farewell but remained behind in the sitting room weighed down by the misery of their company.

Is it so much to ask that my family have faith in me?

She closed her eyes, fighting for her calm and equilibrium. She almost wished the constant scolding and reprimands made her angry. That, at least, would propel her onward. Instead, she was always left with a heavy heart, feeling broken and unsure of herself.

"Your family are utter louts." Artemis's voice echoed from the far corner, amongst a grouping of chairs that had their backs to the rest of the room. From her chair, Artemis rose and walked toward her. "I was engrossed in a book and didn't realize until it was too late that I was, essentially, eavesdropping on a private moment." She sat on the sofa beside Ellie. "I decided interrupting and revealing my presence would be *more* embarrassing than hiding in the corner and waiting."

"Is it so pathetic that I just want them to . . . like me?" Ellie felt ridiculous speaking the words out loud.

"I think that makes you very human and not at all pathetic."

Ellie let her head drop against the back of the sofa. "I should just pack up my things and return home."

"Now *that* would be pathetic." Artemis took Ellie's hand and pulled her up from the sofa. "I can see we have work to do."

"What do you mean?"

Artemis grinned at her, then released Ellie's hand and walked at her side, waving her along when Ellie fell behind. Their path took them to the guest bedchamber Ellie was using.

A woman stood inside whom Ellie had never seen before. Her deep-brown hair was pulled up in a perfectly executed chignon with a bright-red ribbon threaded throughout and just the perfect number of loose tendrils allowed to frame her face. Her dress of deepest blue, with red embroidered flowers, was more fashionable than lady's maids were generally known to wear. Ellie knew there were no other guests staying in the home, and she did not think Artemis had received a caller. Who, then, was this unknown woman?

"Ellie, this is Rose," Artemis said. "She is a genius in matters of fabrics, color combinations, and accessorizing."

"Is she one of the Huntresses?" Ellie asked.

Rose twisted her mouth in disapproval. "Hardly."

Artemis laughed. "Rose is far closer to being Leto than one of Artemis's band."

Ellie shook her head. "You will never convince me Rose is old enough to be your mother."

A slow smile spread over Rose's face. "I like you, Miss Ellie. I like you very much indeed."

Though Ellie did not know many people from India and had only rarely heard their flavor of English, there was no mistaking Rose hailed from that area of the world.

"Do you like Ellie enough to help me undo the damage her mother has done to her fashionability?" Artemis asked.

"I am neither Leto nor a miracle worker," Rose said. "What I am is exceptionally good at what I do."

Ellie knew her parents would reprimand her for being too outspoken, but she pushed ahead with the question she was desperate to have answered. "And what is it, precisely, that you do?"

"I am Artemis's lady's maid."

Ellie's surprise must have shown.

Artemis grew a bit stiff. "Do you disapprove of a woman from India acting as a lady's maid?"

"Not at all." Ellie looked to Rose, hoping she had not given offense. "I was surprised only because you are dressed so fashionably, and I do not believe I have ever encountered a lady's maid who was so incredibly *à la mode*."

Rose acknowledged that with a dip of her head. "That is not the most common objection I hear, you understand."

"I can imagine," Ellie said.

Artemis relaxed, her expression turning a little less warrior-like. She had clearly been ready to do battle.

Rose, apparently satisfied with Ellie's explanation, crossed to the clothes press and pulled open the doors containing Ellie's rather pathetic wardrobe. "This is what I have to work with, is it?"

"Sadly, yes," Artemis said. "And, of course, anything amongst my clothing that you think might be useful. Mrs. Lancaster has made the same offer."

"I don't wish to take clothes from your sister-in-law," Ellie objected.

"It will give her an excuse to procure something new," Artemis said. "My brother informs me she is forever insisting no money be spent on her. Breaks his heart. If we use anything of hers, she will not be able to deny him the opportunity to spoil her a little."

It was one of the most endearing things Ellie had ever heard said about a husband in regard to his wife. How could her parents not want her to marry someone who adored her that much? How different her life would be than the one she would live if married to a man who cared nothing for her.

"What you selected for her yesterday was quite flattering," Rose said. "Though I still maintain that more gold threading and a larger selection of bold colors would do English fashion a world of good." She spoke in a tone that clearly indicated this was not the first time the topic had been raised between them.

"I do not disagree with you, but we have to work within the confines we have been given." Artemis pulled out an armful of Ellie's dresses, which amounted to all of them, and laid them on the bed. "Undermining assumptions requires finesse."

"For some assumptions, there is not enough finesse in all the world," Rose said.

Artemis didn't argue. She motioned to the pile of dresses. "Which of these is salvageable, do you think?"

The two began evaluating every piece of outer clothing Ellie had. Realizing she was not necessary to the endeavor, Ellie lowered herself into the chair near the window and waited. Part of her felt a bit left out, but listening to these women who knew vastly more than she did on such a complicated topic was fascinating.

They spoke of trims and necklines and silhouettes. They waxed long and deep about fabrics and patterns. The dresses were sorted into piles Artemis and Rose seemed to both understand but that were a complete mystery to Ellie.

Rose stepped out of the room at one point. Artemis didn't turn her attention to Ellie but kept up her examination and evaluation of the dresses on the bed before her.

"My figure is not particularly suited to current fashions," Ellie said. "That will likely present you significant difficulties."

"Is that something your mother has said to you?" Artemis asked, eyeing one of Ellie's gowns closely.

"Frequently."

Artemis looked over her shoulder at her. "The styles she has chosen for you are not the right ones for you. They do not flatter your figure."

"Can anything?" Ellie tried not to be overly sensitive about her more ample proportions, but she was not unaware of them.

That brought Artemis around fully, looking at her as if she'd just grown a second nose. "Of course. Oh, Ellie, any number of fashionable silhouettes and cuts would look marvelous on you."

"I'm not exactly slender. And I'm rather short. That combination is not one likely to earn me any accolades."

"You wait until Rose and I have your dresses sorted," Artemis said, turning back to the dresses on the bed. "You'll realize that height and slimness do not define beauty. The right clothing makes a world of difference."

Ellie felt a little better. "You enjoy this."

A satisfied smile spread across Artemis's face. "I enjoy few things more than designing and creating a wardrobe. Sadly, it is not a profession open to a lady. Though I would dearly love to do it more, I dare not press my luck too far."

"Because 'undermining assumptions requires finesse'?"

Artemis's expression turned quieter and a little wearier. "And more patience than I fear I have."

Rose returned in the next moment, three gowns hung over one arm and several lengths of ribbon, lace, and other trims draped over the other. "If you have *any* patience, I would be quite surprised."

Artemis exchanged an amused look with Ellie. "Do you see why I think of her as Leto? Only a mother would dare be so blunt."

"She's far kinder than my mother," Ellie said. "Would you consider adopting me, Rose? Or taking on the role of older sister? I also have a less-than-ideal one of those."

"Promise you will be better behaved than Artemis, and I will accept."

The two women were soon fully engrossed once more in the matter of Ellie's wardrobe. They worked remarkably well together, both quickly understanding each other's ideas and visions. How long had Rose been acting in the capacity of Artemis's lady's maid? Either they had known each other a long time to allow such familiarity, or they were simply remarkably well-matched.

Whatever the history there, Ellie was grateful for the two of them. Though she couldn't be certain they were motivated by concern for her more than their love of fashion, she was still unspeakably happy they were helping her.

CHAPTER TWELVE

NEWTON HAD LAUGHED OUT LOUD when Charlie had read him the summons he had received from Artemis. "Summons" truly was the only way to describe the letter. Artemis Lancaster never did do things by half. Their presence, the note said, was required at the Lancaster house for a clandestine venture of utmost importance. Seeing as the last plot he'd been invited to join had been the courtship with Ellie, he was beside himself with anticipation about what this latest development would be.

Henson answered the door with as little pomposity as ever. Perhaps someday when Newton had a place of his own, he would find himself a butler exactly like this ragamuffin one.

How odd it was that he found himself so delighted to be in this house when he severely disliked being in his parents' house. Family ought to be the people with whom one was the most at ease, the most happy. Based on Ellie's explanation of her own family as well as his observations of them, he suspected she would not have found that to be true either. He worried about her, especially after the note she had received from her parents. Artemis had promised to prevent Ellie's required return home, and Newton hoped Ellie was happy as a permanent guest in someone else's home.

They were deposited in the usual sitting room with the usual lack of explanation. They knew from experience that Henson understood what came next, but he didn't always acknowledge that he knew. He would learn in time.

"What do you think this latest scheme is?" Charlie asked. "Considering Artemis appears to be at the helm of it, I find myself rather terrified."

"And yet you came so willingly," Newton said. "You make quite a show of disliking her, but I find myself beginning to suspect that Miss Sham-caster does not meet with your disapproval as much as you have indicated she has."

"I do not wholly disapprove of her," Charlie said. "I simply do not mind-lessly admire her as so many do."

"When one considers the kindness she has shown our new friend Ellie and her sincere embracing of the Huntresses—young ladies often in difficult circumstances—then, no matter that she is a bit bold and brash in her approach, one cannot genuinely argue that she is not worthy of admiration."

Charlie sighed. "I am not unaware of her good qualities."

Interesting. "Then why do you feel such animosity toward her?"

"Because she is disingenuous. She's playing a part, and in a way one does not generally see in Society. Most people assume more stiff and unyielding manners when mingling with the *ton*, but she takes the role-playing much further than that. Her mask is more than mere politeness; it is deceptive, intentionally and unnecessarily so. I can't like that."

Newton kept his peace. Charlie's oldest brother played a role as well, that of a dandy. Some of the persona seemed quite real. He clearly had a flair for fashion and had a remarkable sense of humor. He seemed to take great delight in absurdity. But there was an aspect of it that even a minimally discerning eye would recognize as being assumed. It seemed best, though, not to point that out. Charlie had a bit of a difficult connection with his family, a tension despite his very real love of them. It was possible that struggle influenced his reaction to their mutual friend.

The lady herself arrived in the room in the next moment. As usual, she wore an expression of such deep-seated mischief Newton couldn't help but smile. He'd done that more and more often the past weeks. It was a change in him, a change that he liked.

Charlie stood quietly, watching Artemis with an expression Newton at first interpreted as unmitigated disapproval. But looking more closely, evaluating more deeply, he could see there was something else in his eyes. Charlie wasn't entirely sure what to make of Artemis. He spoke as if he had decided the entirety of her character, but that wasn't the case at all. Charlie was still trying to sort her out.

"What scheme have you thought up this time?" Newton asked.

Artemis sat. They followed suit.

"Not a scheme," Artemis said. "I need your help."

"Help?" Charlie asked, disbelief ringing in the single word. "I didn't think goddesses ever needed help with anything."

"Well, this is a task for mere mortals. So I thought immediately of you."

Charlie leaned back in his chair. "Typical."

Newton thought it best to head off any squabble before it began. "What is it you need us to do?"

"Practice."

He suspected Artemis made the mysterious pronouncement on purpose. She did enjoy drama.

"Practice *what*, precisely?" he asked.

"I am tutoring someone who is in need of practicing what she is learning."

That wasn't any more illuminating than her much shorter pronouncement a moment earlier.

"I'm afraid we are going to need more information," Newton said.

Artemis waved that off. "It really is quite simple. A young lady needs a bit of practice being more astute in the ways of Society, more bold in advocating for herself. I've been helping her understand the intricacies of that. While she *is* learning a great deal, nothing can take the place of actual practice. And I knew the two of you would be kind to her while she is learning."

It was an unlooked-for compliment. Newton didn't consider himself particularly savvy in social matters. And Charlie never received a compliment from her ever.

"You are not doing this as some sort of a joke, are you?" Charlie asked. "I won't be part of an effort to embarrass some poor soul simply for your entertainment."

The dramatics dropped away on the instant. A flush of angry color touched Artemis's cheek. "I know you do not think highly of me, Mr. Jonquil, but I'm not a monster, and I never inflict pain on vulnerable people. Not ever."

Charlie nodded, though whether he was truly convinced or simply wishing to move on with the undertaking, Newton couldn't decide.

"We will most certainly help," Newton said.

"I was hopeful you would," Artemis said. "My protégé will be down in only a moment."

Ellie must've known about this undertaking as well. She couldn't live in the same house and not be aware of such a project. Footsteps sounded just outside the door. Newton rose, as did Charlie.

The person who entered wasn't a stranger, nor a put-upon tragic lady at the mercy of a cruel joke. Ellie herself stepped inside. She was dressed in a lovely pink-and-white striped gown he didn't think he'd seen her wear before. She looked lovely in it.

Her dress was not the only thing new about her. Something different had been done with her hair. It was somehow both simpler and more elegant than the way she'd worn it before. He liked it very much indeed.

"Ellie." Artemis waved her inside. "Charlie and Newton have agreed, just as I assured you they would."

"Are you horribly embarrassed on my behalf?" she asked them.

Charlie's kind heart showed in that moment. His expression was empathetic without being pitying. "There is nothing to be embarrassed about. You are a dear friend, Ellie. I will gladly help you whenever and however you wish me to."

Ellie smiled softly. Newton was pleased to see it but wished it were directed at him.

"She hardly needs tutoring in how to navigate in Society," Charlie said. "She has done perfectly well every time I've been in company with her."

Artemis nodded. "I haven't been teaching her to function; I've been helping her be more herself, more *boldly* herself."

"I don't understand." Newton addressed the remark to both ladies.

Ellie answered. "My family has a tendency to berate me into hiding and keeping silent." She looked to Charlie. "I don't think I said a word to you during your visit to Shropshire last year. I was too terrified, not of *you* but of my family, who made me too afraid to say a thing. The few times I have dared to be myself, I've been quite thoroughly scolded. It was far safer to hide myself away."

How well Newton related to that sentiment. His family was forever pushing him into silence as well.

"First, Ellie, I think we should practice witty conversation," Artemis said.

"Ellie is already witty," Newton objected.

Artemis gave him such a melodramatically dry look, they all laughed. Newton did not use to do that so easily. "I didn't say she needed to practice being witty; she simply needs to allow that wit to shine in conversation. Ladies are too often told they should make themselves seem deeply stupid when talking with . . . well, with *anyone*, really. But with practice, being herself will come more naturally."

Ellie appeared to be enjoying herself, which made participating in the practice all the more appealing. Artemis motioned for her to begin a conversation.

"We have been enjoying very mild weather of late," she said.

Artemis didn't object to the commonplace conversation starter.

Charlie assumed a languid posture. He fussed with the cuffs of his jacket, his expression both a bit arrogant and a significant amount urbane. "Excellent weather when one wishes to be seen to advantage, as one always ought."

It was an absolutely perfect impression of his dandified oldest brother. So bang up to the mark, in fact, that the other three burst into laughter. He raised a brow, another affectation of the earl's, and they were lost in mirth once more.

Over the course of their witty conversation practice, Charlie amazed the ladies with his remarkable talent for mimicry. Newton had known him too long to not already be acquainted with that side of him. He played roles ranging from Artemis's infamous brother-in-law to the Prince Regent himself. He had the group in such a constant state of merriment that any nervousness Ellie might have felt would have most certainly melted away.

Indeed, she was soon so at ease that she leaned toward Newton now and then, bumping him with her shoulder, smiling up at him, sparkling with joy. His smile never faded; it couldn't. Her happiness filled his own heart with pleasure.

She adroitly waved off the horrified and scandalized reactions the three of them sometimes chose. Though the real-life versions of these lessons would not be so ridiculous, Newton could already see the benefit in them. One was far less intimidated by a situation one had made jest of again and again.

"Now," Artemis said after a hilarious quarter hour of pretended conversations. "Let us role-play the receiving of compliments and responses to insults."

"I am not willing to insult her," Newton said firmly. "Even in jest."

That earned him looks of approval from the ladies. Charlie, however, pretended to be sick to his stomach, which earned him a not-entirely-playful swat on the arm from Artemis.

"The 'insults' will be too ridiculous to be hurtful," Artemis assured Newton. "Allow me to demonstrate." She twisted her features into a sour expression and hunched a little, a well-executed portrayal of the sort of ill-tempered dragon one encountered throughout Society. "Why, Miss Ellie," she said, speaking through her nose, "how brave of you to wear that particular shade of yellow. Not all young ladies have the fortitude to go about looking as though they are suffering from a liver complaint."

Ellie was not wearing yellow, which made the observation entirely farcical.

Ellie's brow pulled in thought. "For insults, you said, 'Retreat, wield my shield, or return fire.'"

"War terminology?" Charlie asked.

"Being a young lady in Society means being constantly under attack," Artemis said. "Battle tactics suit the situation horrifyingly well."

That sent Newton's heart to his toes. He looked to Ellie. She offered a small nod.

"I'm sorry." He set his hand around hers. "I hope Artemis's tactics make life in the *ton* a little easier to endure."

"I think they will."

"I am curious what her approaches look like when applied," Newton said.

Ellie kept their fingers entwined. It felt as natural as breathing.

"Retreat means that the insult is, essentially, ignored. Wielding my shield means that I deflect the insult, usually by changing the topic of conversation."

Both excellent tactics depending on the situation.

"And return fire isn't, as I first thought, to insult the person in return," Ellie said.

"Although sometimes that is too tempting to avoid." Artemis nodded subtly with her head toward Charlie, eyes pulled wide in theatrical emphasis.

Ellie smiled as she continued her explanation. "To 'return fire,' in this instance, means to stand my ground, to speak in my own defense, to make quite clear to all those within earshot that what was said was not acceptable and no one of manners or civility would think otherwise."

That was bold by anyone's standards.

"I think returning fire will be the most difficult to do," Ellie said. "We are taught quite specifically that a young lady does not take a stand in her own defense. Our required response is to sit in silence and endure whatever is flung at us."

He'd chosen that approach, more or less, with his parents. What must it be like to have that approach required of oneself in *all* situations?

"What is your response to Antique Artemis's observation of your fictionally sallow complexion?" Charlie asked.

Ellie stiffened her posture and tipped her chin upward. "And I applaud your bravery in going about with spectacles that clearly do not work as well as they ought."

They dissolved in a heap of laughter. She had chosen "return fire" and had managed it brilliantly. On and on, they practiced. Newton took up the offering of compliments, leaving the admittedly absurd insults to Charlie and Artemis. Ellie proved herself adept at it all.

"The real test, of course, will be if I can maintain this when next I encounter my parents or my sister." Though Ellie didn't seem to have lost her confidence, there was some uncertainty there. "Something about hearing *their* disapproval, in particular, simply takes the wind out of my sails."

Artemis laughed. "You have been in this house too long, Ellie. You are beginning to speak in naval terms."

"If Rose has her say, I will also begin decrying the bland and boring fashion of this 'dreary island.'"

Newton didn't know who Rose was, but he liked that Ellie had gained yet another friend.

Friend.

He knew that was how she viewed him, no matter that he'd held her hand for a time. Their "courtship" was a ruse, after all, one he had agreed to. He'd gone along both as an entertainment and a favor. It had all been fun and harmless when they'd first begun.

It felt less so now. He didn't want to abandon their scheme. He wanted it to be real.

Heaven help him, he wanted it to be real.

CHAPTER THIRTEEN

ELLIE ALWAYS FELT A LITTLE nervous when making her way to a Society function. She had spent far too many years listening to her family list the ways in which she had made a mull of her time amongst the *ton* to be unaware of the myriad mistakes that awaited her. Leaving for a ball in the company of Artemis and her brother and sister-in-law was an entirely different experience.

Her nervousness leaned more toward anticipation this time. She was excited and hopeful. Rose had taken extra time the evening before, helping Ellie choose a gown and decide on a suitable hairstyle. Artemis's boldness lessons had continued in preparation for this first outing. Ellie felt prepared to make what was essentially a debut in Society. Never mind that she had attended many events before; she was finally attending one as her true self.

She stepped into Artemis's bedchamber, where Rose was helping with the final ministrations.

"Have we overlooked anything? Anything we need to change?" Ellie watched the inarguable experts in these things, hopeful that she really was ready.

"You look a vision," Rose said.

She was never effusive with her praise, but she was also never unkind. Ellie felt certain Rose would not tell her she looked well if she didn't but, rather, would fix whatever was amiss. Artemis was equally dependable. The two really were remarkable. It was indeed a shame Society did not allow ladies to take up dressmaking and designing. These two could easily be the most sought-after mantua-makers in the entire kingdom.

Artemis was soon ready to leave, and Rose motioned them away before turning back toward the tools she had set out for fixing Artemis's hair.

"Do you suppose Rose wishes she could go with us to these events?" Ellie asked. "It seems such a shame she did so much work but is not able to participate in the larks that her efforts made possible."

"I have actually asked her," Artemis said. "She told me there are times when she wishes she could go. She would like to see all of the ladies in their finery and observe for herself the intricacies and functioning of English fashion. She said she would also enjoy dancing or deep conversations about the matters of the day. But she also said she finds Society quite obnoxious and, therefore, doesn't feel she's being denied too much. She much prefers the company of her close friends."

"Does she not consider you a close friend?"

"I hope that she does." Artemis's tone turned uncharacteristically somber. "That is a difficult thing to know, and not merely because Rose is, in many ways, quite unreadable. Our differing circumstances and the fact that she, if we are being quite technical, works for me, puts a barrier between us. I have seen others develop close connections to their abigails and valets. I have some hope that we can develop that as well."

Ellie did not at all know how to navigate the complexities of human relations, but she wanted to understand them better.

They were attending the Fancy Ball at the Upper Assembly Rooms that evening. It was a familiar enough social event for her to not be overly worried about what would happen and what was expected. Unfortunately, her family nearly always attended. She likely would not be able to entirely avoid them.

Arriving in the company of the Lancasters was quite a boon to Ellie. People who had hardly noticed her before greeted her with deference. It was unexpected, unfamiliar, and absolutely welcome. When she felt a little intimidated, she called upon Artemis's tutoring and upon pretending to feel confident even when she did not. She suspected she was doing well. No one seemed to look askance at her.

Within five minutes of each other, the Huntresses arrived and joined their group. Artemis's brother and his wife had gone to speak with their own set. That was one of the joys of being part of Artemis's band: freedom Ellie hadn't ever known before.

"You look breathtaking," Gillian said. "I suspect Rose had a hand in this transformation."

Ellie smiled and nodded. Apparently, she was not the first to benefit from the expertise and generosity of that woman.

"Rose and Artemis are the reason I prefer a rounded neckline and will never wear pale pink," Daria said with a laugh. "Imagine my horror upon realizing that I had, for two Seasons in a row, looked as though I had spent long hours bonnetless under a hot desert sun, thanks to that color choice."

They all laughed at that, though not so loudly as to be inappropriate. Mother and Lillian would have declared any degree of laughter entirely ill-mannered. How grateful Ellie was to discover they were wrong.

They continued their circuit of the ballroom. Gentlemen stopped them now and then to request the honor of dancing with them. That was also an experience Ellie was unaccustomed to but found she very much liked. Only after having agreed to stand up for three sets did she cross paths with the one gentleman she truly wished to dance with.

Newton, as always, was there in the company of Charlie. Ellie had always dreamed of having a companion like that. She was so pleased that she finally had not merely one but three.

"You look beautiful tonight," Newton said. "I wish I understood more about fashion so I could offer you a more detailed compliment. I feel all I am able to say is that you are quite stunning."

The compliment was more effusive than Ellie had ever before received. It might even have been considered a bit too bold by the harshest of sticklers. She, however, loved it.

Newton requested the honor of standing up with her during the Roger de Coverley. She readily and wholeheartedly accepted.

"I do not know what the Lancasters are thinking, allowing Miss Lancaster and her guests to accept invitations from young gentlemen without requiring those invitations be approved by them first." She cringed at the sound of her mother's voice coming from directly behind her.

Ellie pasted a smile on her face and turned around. There stood her father, mother, and Lillian. All seemed surprised to discover Ellie was among the group Mother had just spoken ill of. Surely, they knew she was one of Artemis's guests.

"Ellie," Mother said. "I did not realize you were there."

"I recognized your voice," Ellie said.

Mother would know now that her disparaging remark had been overheard. A moment passed in which she didn't offer any apology or cover for her unkind words now that she knew who had been their recipient.

A publicly offered insult. Ellie knew her three options.

"Mr. Hughes is well known to Mr. and Mrs. Lancaster," Ellie said. "He is a regularly invited and welcomed guest in their home. As they have never deemed to cast aspersions on his character, I can only imagine what more approval would be required for him to meet with the approval of anyone else."

Her family's surprise only grew. Newton had turned toward them as she'd spoken, likely having heard his name. Charlie and Artemis looked on as well.

"I would never speak ill of Mr. Hughes's character." Lillian cast him a look of pleading. She often employed an expression and posture of demure distress when hoping to gain the notice of a gentleman. Did she think that was what Newton hoped for, a lady incapable of doing anything?

Newton showed tremendous forbearance, but Ellie suspected he was reaching the end of his patience with her family. She truly hoped he didn't number her among them any longer. No matter that their connection began as a pretended one; she did not wish him to think poorly of her.

"And, Mr. Jonquil," Mother said, turning to Charlie, "we, of course, did not wish to imply that you were an objectionable partner for any young lady. Our Elfrida too often neglects the manners we taught her to have. I assure you, we did teach her."

In typical fashion, her mother had assuaged her own embarrassment by blaming and belittling Ellie. Ever the scapegoat. Ever the failure.

"Perhaps it would be best if you spent the remainder of the evening near us," Father said to Ellie. He did not look angry but embarrassed.

Why was it her family was always ashamed of her even when she toed the line with exactness? She was never made to feel that way at the Lancaster home. Newton treated her as though her company were a gift and an honor.

Between his support and Artemis's boldness lessons, Ellie felt equal to the task of defending herself properly to her parents. "While I appreciate the offer, I will remain in the company of the family who brought me here this evening. The Lancasters have been everything that is gracious and kind, and I will not repay their goodness with the insult of thoughtless abandonment."

It was the sort of articulately expressed, thinly veiled criticism Artemis excelled at. "Returning fire" with subtle precision.

"I'm certain the Lancasters realize we meant no disrespect." Mother watched Artemis with a look of worry.

Lillian was just as ill at ease. She had shown more signs of uncertainty in the brief time Ellie and Artemis had been friends than she had all her life before that. It was an odd thing to see. Not satisfying or pleasant. Ellie loved her sister despite their difficulties, but Lillian needed to understand that she could not treat people as poorly as she often did, and neither could she use them as pawns in her intricate game of living chess.

"Do not allow me to keep you," Ellie said. She hoped it wasn't too obvious she was doing her best impression of Artemis.

They had rehearsed dismissals so many times. It fell under the category of "retreat." Artemis had made quite clear that retreat was not to be confused with failure. When utilized strategically, stepping back was its own kind of victory.

Her family nodded and offered unexceptional words of farewell, then went on their way. Ellie could hardly believe it had gone so well. She couldn't remember the last time a public scolding from her family had not led to much more vicious reprimands. She began to feel she had found her escape.

Charlie offered his arm. Ellie accepted.

"That was rather brilliantly done," he said. "It seems all of our rehearsal is proving efficacious."

Ellie both sighed and smiled. The relief she felt grew and grew. She had been nervous at the thought of being firm and unbending with her parents. But doing the thing right, as Artemis often said, made all the difference.

"Perhaps I ought to take a few lessons from Artemis," Newton said, walking on the opposite side of Charlie. "If I could end my parents' complaints against me as well as you just did, it would change everything for me."

"I have not ever seen you interact with your parents," she said to him. "Do they treat you the way mine treat me?"

Newton shook his head. "They are not truly scolding or berating. They simply disapprove."

Charlie offered a bit of wisdom in his remarkable imitation of his eccentric brother. "Should we cross paths with them tonight, remember: retreat, wield your shield, or return fire. That is the trick of it." He slipped his arm from Ellie's and turned, offering her a deferential bow. "Now, if you will excuse me, I mean to retreat before our Boldness Boss comes over to critique my performance this evening."

With a jaunty step in a path the exact opposite direction of Artemis, Charlie slipped away.

"It is a shame they don't value each other's company," Ellie said. "They are both such genuinely good people."

"Good, yes, but both quite stubborn," Newton said.

Ellie looked up at him. "They might find they could be good friends. We have become just that."

He took her hand and slipped it through his arm. "Very good friends, indeed."

His words warmed her. And yet, she felt a twinge of disappointment. They were friends, and she was grateful for that. Her feelings, though, tiptoed beyond friendship. She wasn't entirely certain what to do with that realization.

They had not resumed their circuit of the room long when she felt Newton tense.

"What has happened?" she asked quietly.

"My parents have arrived." He motioned subtly toward a sophisticated couple coming in their direction. Had he not identified them as his mother and father, she would likely have been able to guess. There was a resemblance in him to both of them.

"Would it be best if I stepped away?" she asked.

"I would appreciate having you here for moral support," he said. "But I also do not wish for you to be made uncomfortable. I will defer to whichever you prefer."

She squared her shoulders. "I will not abandon you."

A nearly invisible but heartwarming change came over him. He stood a little taller, a little more confidently, and he watched his parents' approach with less uncertainty.

"Good evening, Mother and Father," he greeted. "I had hoped to see you here this evening."

"We had hoped to see you," his mother said. "You are so seldom home. It seems the Upper Assembly Rooms are the only place we see you any longer."

While it was something of a complaint, it was not offered in the same tone of insult Ellie's family used.

"I have been enjoying myself," Newton said. "When you suggested earlier that I enjoy Bath and take advantage of the society here, I confess I balked a little. I'm grateful now to have been pushed toward it."

Ellie nodded inwardly. He had quite expertly wielded his shield, shifting the complaint to a compliment.

"Pleased to hear it," his father said. The elder Mr. Hughes looked to Ellie briefly. "I believe you are Miss Elfrida Napper."

Newton immediately jumped into the gap. "Forgive me. I have neglected introductions. Mother, Father, this is, indeed, Miss Elfrida Napper of Shropshire. Miss Ellie, these are my parents, Mr. and Mrs. Hughes."

Bows and curtsies accompanied the expected greetings.

"I had hoped to come here to see you dancing with Miss Lancaster," Mrs. Hughes said. "You seem to have developed a friendship and connection with her. She's quite an exceptional young lady."

"We have indeed formed a friendship," Newton said. "I have missed the company of my sisters since they were married. In Miss Lancaster, I have found something of that connection again."

More redirection expertly deployed.

His parents hesitated but a moment.

His father took up the discussion. "Miss Lancaster has a significant group of companions. Have all of them come to take on the role of sister in your mind?"

"I find myself far less heartbroken at the infrequency of my interactions with my sisters. And I find myself no longer lacking for Society. I'm pleased to report your plans have gone excellently."

Newton was doing remarkably well. Artemis's tutoring in boldness had benefited him also.

"Now if you'll excuse me," he said, "I hear the opening strains of the Roger de Coverley, and I have promised that dance."

His mother's expression turned intrigued. "To whom have you promised it?"

Newton set his hand on hers. "To Miss Ellie."

He left no opportunity for objections but simply walked away as if he had all the right in the world to do so. He did, of course. Parents often forgot that their children, once grown, deserved to have the living of their own lives.

"That was quite well done, Newton," she whispered. "If you and I are not careful, we will find ourselves considered people capable of deciding our own futures."

"Futures free of unwanted masks, I hope."

Masks. Was not the ruse they had been enacting one of masks and make-believe? And he wished specifically to be free of that. She had been so grateful when he'd agreed to join her in their little scheme. She felt certain she'd found an ingenious means of escape.

It was beginning to feel like a trap.

CHAPTER FOURTEEN

NEWTON'S INTERACTION WITH HIS PARENTS the night before had gone better than he could have imagined. It made him wonder why he hadn't tried to speak up for himself previously. He, of course, knew the reason: he had been a coward.

When he was a child, he had desperately feared stepping out of line and disappointing his parents in any way. That worry had stayed with him all these years, leaving him convinced he had to accept the options they offered him. To place his wisdom above theirs felt unforgivably arrogant. He'd assumed he would live his life trying to find happiness in whatever they prescribed.

Ellie's willingness to undermine her parents' demands and eventually stand up to them directly had shown him what bravery looked like.

In his newfound confidence, he began thinking differently about his future. He wanted to pursue the law, and he knew without a doubt that doing so was well within the realm of acceptable behavior. His parents would rather he didn't, but that didn't make it improper.

"Would you like me to have Jason send his response here or to your family estate in the country?" Charlie asked. He was placing his personal effects into the small portmanteau he meant to take with him on his journey to London. He needed to return to Cambridge and was doing so by way of Town.

Newton, in an act of borderline audacity, had asked a favor of his friend: to deliver a missive to his brother, the barrister, and ask him to respond.

"Ask him to send it here. I will be here for the next two weeks, and I would prefer to receive the letter before I embark on my own trip to London, if possible."

"Do you truly mean to begin your study of the law regardless of your parents' dictates?" Charlie closed his traveling bag.

"Ellie and Artemis convinced me. They are quite persuasive."

"I will allow the descriptor where Ellie is concerned, but Artemis is nothing short of pushy."

Newton laughed. Even Charlie smiled. His animosity toward their friend was showing more cracks. The two would likely never be on entirely friendly terms, but Newton hoped they would at least find a degree of neutrality between them.

"Thank you again for your willingness to deliver my letter to your brother. I do think he could help my parents come around to embracing my way of doing things." That was his plan.

"If anyone can make a persuasive argument, it is Jason," Charlie said. "He was always meant to be a barrister. No one can make a case better than he can."

Newton wasn't depending on Jason to convince them before he pursued his dreams. He simply hoped to add one more brick to the foundation before setting off and claiming his future.

He walked with Charlie from the guest bedchamber his friend had been using down to the front of the house. Having Charlie's company had been an absolute highlight of his time in Bath. He had tried to convince Charlie to come to London during term break in the spring, too, but Charlie, true to character, did not have much of a desire to do so.

During their holiday here in Bath, Newton had solved one of Charlie's mysteries: the reason for his animosity toward Artemis. Now if only he knew the reason for Charlie's dislike of London.

He saw Charlie off. Things would be different between them moving forward. They would no longer be in school together, something that had been true for only one year of the past seven. Life would take them in different directions now. Change was a good thing, but it was also difficult. Somehow, Newton needed to convince him to come to Town, if not for the social whirl, then at least to spend a little time together.

Newton found himself restless, unable to remain at home. And though he was feeling more confident where his parents were concerned, he wasn't particularly in the mood for a confrontation. So he set his feet to the pavement and began to walk. He told himself he was aiming for the Gravel Walk, but his steps took him, instead, to the Lancasters' house.

Henson showed him inside with a little more finesse than he usually employed. The man was learning his job. Newton hoped Henson never became truly stodgy. That would be a shame.

"I would like to visit with Miss Lancaster and Miss Ellie," Newton said when the man neglected to ask for whom he had called. Henson nodded but seemed a little unsure what to do next.

"You can wait in the sitting room," Henson said. "I'll go ask what's to be done."

Upon entering the sitting room, Newton discovered it was not empty. Lillian Napper sat inside.

Newton kept relatively near to the ajar door. No maid was present, no parent, no sign of the master or mistress of the house. Ellie's sister had shown herself to be quite single-minded and unlikely to give up easily on something she wanted. Newton knew with perfect and alarming clarity that one of the things she currently wished for was an advantageous match with him on account of his family's connections and coffers.

"Do you need to stand uncomfortably far across the room?" the lady inquired with sweetness that did not ring true.

"I assure you, I am not the least uncomfortable in my current location," he said. "Henson has gone to quickly ask a question. I am remaining only until I receive that answer."

She could not have missed the lack of intimacy in his response, though she showed no signs of being discouraged. Indeed, she lifted a shoulder a little, watching him with head slightly tilted. It was the practiced pose of a young lady hoping to lure a gentleman closer. How little she knew him. He remained near the door and did his utmost to show no signs of interest.

"I was pleased to see you at the Fancy Ball last evening," she said. "I must confess myself deeply disappointed to not have the opportunity to dance with you."

Newton would not be shamed into committing himself to a dance in the future. "I found myself engaged for every set," he said. "The ladies, you will remember, far outnumbered the gentlemen. Such is too often the case, even though we are no longer in a time of active warfare."

"I do hope should such a thing be once again true, you will reserve a dance for me."

"'Should such a thing happen again?'" he asked, feigning confusion. "A return to war? Heaven forbid."

Her eyes narrowed the tiniest bit, as if she were attempting to sort him out. "No, of course not. I meant a ball at which the gentlemen are outnumbered."

"Ah." He nodded but made no commitment, what Artemis would have deemed "retreat."

Lillian Napper, though, was not the sort to be distracted. "I saw that you found time to dance with my sweet younger sister. It has been nice to see her taken under wing by somebody. The poor thing has no experience in Society.

We have resigned ourselves to knowing she has found her best home in being someone's compassion project."

If shaming him was a bad tactic, shaming Ellie was a far worse one.

"I am quite honored that your sister thinks me enough of a friend to spend time with me. Indeed, all of Bath has declared her a delightful addition to the Lancasters' list of friends and close associates. Should I cross paths with your parents again, I will make certain to thank them for bringing her here."

Lillian did not seem to miss the importance of his word choice and the slight turn in topic it constituted. "We would love to receive you at our house here in Bath," she said. "We will be home tonight, in fact. We would be delighted to have you come. And Ellie will not be there, so you needn't be worried that you will spend your evening advising the poor thing in how to go about in company."

Retreat had failed. His shield had proven insufficient. There was but one tactic left.

"My parents are quite in demand amongst Society. I cannot remember the last time they had an evening without social obligations. Should they find themselves home tonight without plans, I will mention your invitation." Goodness, he hated sounding so pompous and so pointedly dismissive. But returning fire was the only option remaining.

"I realize it is not considered gentlemanly to openly call on a lady when the connection between them is still in its early stages. As such, I suggested your parents calling so you could have an excuse to come." She moved closer to him. "But I assure you, I am not so fragile as many young ladies. You needn't wait on a pretense to call. I promise you will be received."

He stepped backward as she approached but misjudged the location of the threshold and found his back brushing up against the wall. This could get awkward. "Pretense is not what is preventing me from calling on you, Miss Napper."

Lillian had come quite close now, near enough that he could see the expression in her eyes better than he could a moment ago. She did not look coquettish; she looked nearly frantic.

"Perhaps," he said, "I ought to simply leave my regrets and call later."

"Do you not think it rude to leave me here, abandoned?" Her flirtatious tone was falling horribly short of the mark. "I'm certain Henson will be only a moment longer."

"Why *are* you in here alone?"

"I came to see Ellie, but she is out."

Newton shook his head. "She is whom I came to see. There really is no point remaining if she is gone."

"No point?" She closed nearly all the distance between them. Standing uncomfortably close. Worryingly close. Scandalously close. "It seems almost like fate, don't you think?"

"Fate doesn't hate me *that* much."

Anger flitted instantaneously across her face, disappearing as quickly as it had appeared. "Ellie has no dowry."

"Do *you*?"

A quick flaring of the nostrils. A deep breath. "I do have something she doesn't."

"And what is that?" he asked calmly.

"This situation and the way it would appear to Society." Gone were the flirting and demurity.

He'd been too subtle in his return fire. The time for kid gloves had passed. "Are you threatening me?" he asked in a low and intentional voice.

Again, she shrugged, but the gesture was no longer merely annoying. It was calculated.

"I think you overestimate the strength of your claim," Newton said, "as well as my concern for your standing or mine."

She opened her mouth, but the sound of Ellie's voice sounded first.

"You also overestimate the quietness with which you're making your accusations. I have heard every word and can undermine your assertions."

Lillian's gaze narrowed as she shifted her focus from him to Ellie standing just beyond the door. "You would speak so insultingly of your own sister?"

"If need be."

Newton turned enough to look at his avenging angel. She stood with the firmness and boldness she'd claimed so adamantly she didn't have. No one would doubt it seeing her now. Artemis had hoped to give her a bit of courage. In that moment, Ellie radiated with dauntlessness.

"You are a *younger* sister," Lillian said. "Your word against mine is hardly the firm defense you seem to think it is."

Artemis stepped into view. "And what of mine, Lillian Napper? Does my word hold weight, do you suppose? If you called *me* a liar, do you think that would go well for you?"

Wrapping her dignity around her like a soiled, torn, poorly patched cloak, Lillian swept past them all and, likely, out of the house entirely.

"I was afraid she would do something like this," Ellie said. "But I had hoped she would prove those fears unfounded."

"At least the threat has been eliminated," Newton said.

Ellie looked at him, then Artemis. With a sigh, she said, "I am not at all certain it has been."

CHAPTER FIFTEEN

SHOPPING WITH ARTEMIS AND ROSE was an experience unlike any other. Their discussion on everything from gowns to ribbon to embroidery thread became a lecture on the science of fashion that would rival any offered at Cambridge, if Cambridge offered education on such matters and, further, if they permitted women to *attend*, let alone teach.

Ellie felt like she had learned more in a single afternoon of wandering with them from shop to shop than she had in all her previous years. When she eventually was required to return home to her family, she would do so with a much better idea of how to make a showing for herself, along with knowing how to speak and act in her own defense. Both lessons were proving invaluable.

Whilst her companions spoke at length over which of Artemis's necklaces would look best with a gown made of indigo taffeta, the ribbon meant to match it being what they were shopping for in this particular shop, Ellie became aware of eyes watching *her*. It was not the first time that had happened since they'd been out that afternoon. She understood people's watching Artemis—she was a diamond, by anyone's estimation—but their attention was on her, and the looks she received were a bit unsettling. She didn't feel threatened, by any means, but she felt their gazes. For someone accustomed to being invisible, it was not a terribly comfortable experience.

She met the gaze of two matrons not too far distant. The moment they realized she was watching them in return, they looked away and immediately began whispering. Ellie couldn't overhear their conversation but had a sinking suspicion they were talking about her. This repeated not much later with a different gathering of ladies, this group younger than the first, though a little older than Ellie herself. It had happened at the linendraper's. It had happened at the millinery. She wanted to think she was imagining the stares, but the frequency prevented her from completely dismissing the experiences.

"People are watching you in odd ways," Rose said without preamble. "I have noticed it all morning. And the whispers are quite obvious too."

Somehow Ellie found the confirmation both reassuring and worrisome. "I'd hoped I was imagining it."

"You aren't."

Artemis watched the two of them, a little confused and more than a little concerned.

Rose took up the explanation. "Something about Ellie has captured the curiosity of Society, and not in a way that appears positive."

"What could possibly have happened?" Artemis said. "I have heard no rumors or whispers. And I can think of nothing that has happened that would cause speculation about her. Perhaps they are not unkind glances."

Rose examined a satin ribbon hanging nearby. "I am acquainted enough with disapproving stares and gossip and whispers to recognize them as such when I see them."

Artemis drew Ellie closer to the both of them. Voice lowered, she said, "We will solve this mystery, I promise you. There is nothing that happens in Society that I cannot sort."

"With help," Rose said.

Artemis dipped her head in acknowledgment. "Wade into your river of information, Rose. We'll meet you back at the house."

Rose left without a word or a backward glance.

"She's not upset, is she?" Ellie asked. "I feel like she didn't particularly want to undertake this."

Artemis hooked an arm through Ellie's. "She plays her cards close to the chest, as I once heard my brother-in-law say. I struggled to make sense of her when she first took on this, no doubt, exhausting role. Enduring me every day is no small feat."

Ellie could smile at that. Artemis had such a knack for lightening a situation.

"I've come to know her better," Artemis continued. "She is kindhearted and generous in addition to being, I suspect, an actual genius. She is not one to employ even a single unnecessary word, which can make her seem upset or arrogant, though she is neither."

"You are fond of Rose," Ellie observed.

"She is, in many ways, the person I wish I were." Artemis led Ellie from the shop and directly past a woman who watched her departure with a bit too much interest. Voice lowered, Artemis said, "I *did* notice it that time."

"What do you suppose is behind this?" Ellie asked.

"I haven't the first idea." Still, Artemis walked past the shops with head held high, giving Ellie the confidence to do the same.

They'd not gone far when Daria and Gillian ran them to ground.

"We were chatting during my mother's at-home this afternoon," Daria said without preamble, "and overheard the oddest comment. About Ellie."

Heavens.

Artemis motioned all of them onward. "We'll head for home. On the way, tell us what you heard."

They walked in a clump, though the pavement was not quite wide enough for four abreast. Still, the matter at hand required the effort.

"Mrs. Carter said, 'Ellie Napper always was a little unusual.'" Daria gave them all a significant look. "And she said it in a tone that indicated her memories of Ellie were meant to confirm something happening now, something that could be explained or at least supported by Ellie being 'a little odd.'"

"*Mrs. Carter* has always been a little odd," Ellie muttered.

Artemis nodded. "Odd and a touch vindictive. She used to say the unkindest things about my sister Daphne."

"And while that was not a particularly kind observation," Daria continued, "it was not what sent us to find you."

Oh dear. "What else was said?" Ellie hated to even ask.

"In response to Mrs. Carter, Miss Ramsey said that while she was surprised to hear reports of Ellie's behavior, she supposed there was always a history of such things when one looked back."

That was a strange thing to say. "What 'reports of my behavior'?"

"Neither lady clarified," Gillian said. "And we didn't dare ask."

They'd not quite reached the Lancaster house when Newton came rushing down the pavement toward them. He looked a little distressed. Ellie didn't know if she could endure more bad news, not without at least a moment to guard herself against it.

"Oh, Ellie," he said and not in a tone of being overjoyed. "I've just had a concerning conversation."

"An epidemic of late, it would seem."

He looked to the Huntresses, all of whom allowed their concern to show. Newton sighed. "I had hoped my mother was misinformed."

Horror seized her on the instant. "Your mother?"

Artemis called for a temporary end of the discussion, insisting they focus their energy on reaching her house. "We need to get a grasp on this so we know what to do next."

No one objected. And no one spoke all the way there. Only when they were seated and tea obtained did the discussion resume.

"What did your mother have to say?" Artemis asked.

"She has heard from a friend of hers that there are whispers going about connected to my name," Newton said.

"We knew your feigned courtship might make people wonder a little," Artemis said, "but absolutely nothing that has happened between you should cause enough speculation to be problematic."

Newton shook his head. "Not that sort of connection. The whispers say that Ellie is attempting to dupe me into an understanding. That she is manipulating me, or using her . . . wiles to ensnare me."

She could do nothing but stare agape in silence.

"Her wiles?" Artemis injected a great deal of disbelief into her repetition of that odd bit. She looked to Ellie. "I don't mean any offense, but you are quite possibly one of the sincerest people I know, despite the ruse you've been enacting."

"No offense taken," Ellie said. "I am as shocked as you are."

"And likely only half as shocked as my mother," Newton said. "But she could not entirely dismiss the whispers. She saw me with Ellie at the ball. I expressed to her my preference for Ellie's company and my enjoyment of dancing with her. Nothing was said that would be seen as improper, but there was no doubt left that she and I have come to know each other. It adds kindling to this particularly odd fire."

Gillian had been rather quiet through the discussion, an aura of contemplation not at all uncommon for her. She spoke next. "I cannot think of anything that has happened with Ellie or Newton or the two of them together that would cause this. There must be something else behind it."

"What?" Artemis asked.

"That is the question of the hour," Daria said.

"How can I address these rumors if I don't know where they are originating?" Ellie asked. She was beginning to feel rather desperate. Few young ladies of her low standing could recover from something like this, even with the Lancasters behind her. She would return home in disgrace, and no amount of boldness would save her from the misery her family would inflict on her for that.

Artemis looked to Newton. "Does Charlie not have an opinion on any of this? He generally has no qualms sharing his thoughts on anything and everything."

"Charlie left Bath yesterday," Newton said. "He wanted to spend a little time with a couple of his brothers before resuming his studies."

"He's gone?" Artemis apparently hadn't heard as much.

Newton nodded. Artemis stood and paced away.

The room sat in almost complete silence. Nothing was decided upon, and nothing was solved. Then into the fruitless effort came a source of wisdom: Rose.

She stepped into the room and calmly declared, "I have the entirety of it."

Artemis waved her inside, taking her seat again and motioning for Rose to sit amongst them. No one seemed the least surprised by her appearance there, except for Newton.

Artemis must have realized his confusion, as she took up the explanation immediately. "Mr. Hughes, this is Rose, fashion expert, lady's maid extraordinaire, and, apparently, the world's most capable spy."

Rose dipped her head quickly. Newton returned the gesture with an equally respectful and properly executed bow. Once she was seated, he sat too. All eyes were on Rose. Ellie expected all their ears were as well.

"The rumor is that Ellie is playing Mr. Hughes for a fool," Rose said. "Rumors began circulating yesterday evening. A few questions to the right people, and I discovered where it all began."

How in heaven's name had she discovered so much in such a short amount of time?

Rose's gaze settled on Ellie. "You clearly are not yet acquainted with the extensiveness of the servants' gossip network."

The servants, for all the English upper class dismissed and belittled them, were the lifeblood of this country. Of course they knew what was happening around the city. They always knew.

"Who started this rumor?" Artemis asked. No matter that she gave the impression of being flighty, she was actually quite brilliant and fully focused when she chose to be.

"I was able to trace it back to one household." Rose looked briefly at Ellie before returning her attention to the gathering as a whole. But it was enough to tell Ellie what she needed to know.

"My family's household, by chance?" Ellie asked.

Rose nodded.

"Your parents are behind this rumor?" Despite his difficulties with his own family, Newton sounded quite horrified at the possibility.

"If I had to guess," Ellie said, "I would place the blame not on my parents but on my sister. She was severely displeased with me when she left here yesterday."

Rose stood once more, as did Newton. "It is my understanding the whispers began with your sister. I put a bug in the ear of a few lady's maids that that is likely where it originated and was the result not of truth but of envy. Miss Napper is known to not have made any conquests whilst here, of either the romantic or the friendship variety. It will not be difficult for that information to spread. It will not undo all the damage, but it might at least cast a bit of doubt here and there." Rose turned and stepped out.

Ellie stood and began pacing. She didn't know what to do. Yes, "a little bit of doubt" was not enough to undo what had been done. Vicious gossip circulated far faster than the truth.

"This is a particularly difficult variety of rumor," Gillian said. "Whispers of compromised reputations are often addressed through courtships and proposals. To be clear, I am not suggesting that remedy in this instance. But a courtship or understanding would only add a whisper of truth to the lies. People would assume Newton proposed because Ellie had been successful in her supposed schemes."

Artemis nodded firmly but offered no solution.

Daria spoke next. "But doing absolutely nothing would likely only convince people of the lack of success Ellie was having, not the lack of trying."

Ellie pressed the tips of her fingers to her temples and rubbed, trying to prevent the headache she felt coming on. In the next moment, Newton was standing before her, looking at her with concern.

"What if there is no solution?" she said. "What if Lillian has destroyed my reputation and I have no choice but to return home in disgrace?"

Slowly, giving her the opportunity to voice any objections, Newton reached out and brushed his hand along her arm. The gentleness of his touch inspired an answering ache in her heart. She leaned against him.

"This would add to the rumors, you realize," Newton said.

"No one here will spread any gossip."

He pulled her into a soft and gentle embrace. Ellie could breathe again, despite the worry in her chest. He'd offered no empty words of reassurance, and neither did he attempt to tell her how she ought to feel about the situation. He simply held her, letting her feel and think whatever she chose. It was a degree of confidence few people had ever expressed in her, and he had done so without words.

Artemis faced them all with the bearing of a goddess. Not the tiniest bit of uncertainty showed, not the tiniest bit of hesitation. "We know where this began, and we know what it is. Now we are going to fix it."

Ellie remained in the circle of Newton's arms as he asked quietly, "How?"

"We are Artemis and Huntresses," their fearless leader said. "There is nothing we cannot do."

CHAPTER SIXTEEN

ELLIE STOOD BETWEEN ARTEMIS AND her brother in the front entryway of the very grand house where Newton and his family resided whilst in Bath. She had known he occupied a rung far above her own, but being surrounded by the reality of it was proving a bit intimidating.

"Chin up, Miss Ellie," Mr. Lancaster said. "The Hugheses are not unfeeling people, and Artemis is not compared to a badger for no reason."

"Shut up, Linus," Artemis said, her tone both laughing and annoyed.

The prim and pompous butler informed them that the family was at home to them. That, Ellie decided, was a good omen. Newton's parents might just have easily refused to see them on account of Ellie's presence.

They were led into a formal drawing room, where Mr. and Mrs. Hughes sat perfectly coiffed and togged. Thank the heavens, Ellie's education in manners and civility made greetings, curtsies, and civilities second nature.

Mrs. Hughes proved the perfect hostess, pouring tea for the lot of them and making light conversation while they all settled in. Newton arrived just as the last cup was distributed. He received welcomes and his own tea and was soon situated among them. He chose, to Ellie's delight, the seat nearest hers.

"How are you?" he asked softly.

"Artemis continually tells me that falling to bits is not permitted. So I have no choice but to carry on."

Newton smiled at her over his teacup. "She is a force, our Artemis."

"One I am pleased is being employed in my favor."

That force spoke loudly enough to bring all attention to her. "We have called upon you for a specific purpose, Mr. and Mrs. Hughes," she said. "We know you are not unaware of the current rumors floating about that, in addition to Miss Ellie, involve your son."

Mrs. Hughes nodded. "We are most certainly aware."

Artemis looked to her brother before returning her attention to Newton's parents. "We have a plan."

Mr. Hughes eyed Mr. Lancaster. "Are you privy to this plan?"

"I am, and it is a good one."

That earned nods from both the elder Hugheses. Newton listened intently as well.

Artemis set her teacup down and addressed them all. "We have given great thought to the particular difficulties of this situation. The usual remedies will likely only increase speculation, not to mention forced marriages are seldom happy ones."

"That is true," Mr. Hughes acknowledged.

"We have sorted a means of dispelling the rumors," Artemis said. "The whispers are that Ellie is tricking Newton into spending time with her in order to eventually force an understanding between the two of them. So, we counter the speculation not by addressing the outcome of this supposed effort but by reframing the origins of their connection."

"I don't understand," Newton said.

But Ellie did. "The rumor rests on the belief that I have forced you to keep company with me. If we can undermine *that*, the rest falls to bits."

"Brilliant," Newton whispered.

Artemis took charge again. "Mr. and Mrs. Hughes, if you are willing to help us put forth the alternate explanation, that Miss Ellie is a friend of your family, and stick to that explanation until the whispers die down, I do believe that will save both your son and my dear friend from the ramifications of this ridiculous whispered scandal."

Mr. and Mrs. Hughes exchanged glances but didn't speak out loud. Ellie wasn't familiar enough with them to know if what she was seeing was encouraging or not. One look at Newton gave her hope.

"It is an excellent idea, Miss Lancaster," Mrs. Hughes said. "And the sooner we begin, the better. Mr. Lancaster, I hope you and your wife, sister, and our mutual friend, Miss Ellie, will join our family at the Theatre Royal this evening."

"Excellent." Artemis rose. "We will see you this evening."

If Mr. Lancaster was at all bothered that his younger sister had just answered on his behalf, he showed no indication of it. He had come to support her, not browbeat her, nor seize control of the effort she herself was spearheading. These siblings loved and cared for and respected each other. Ellie wished she could say the same of her sister.

"I believe this will help," Newton said. "We might escape these rumors after all."

Heavens, she hoped so. Because, if it didn't work, she didn't have the first idea what they were going to do.

"I hope all goes well this evening." Rose slipped another pin into Ellie's hair, then stepped back to look her over with a critical eye. "Artemis has a flair for strategy, which ought to give you a measure of confidence."

"*You* have given me a measure of confidence. I likely haven't thanked you enough."

Rose acknowledged Ellie's gratefulness with a quick nod, then adjusted one of the sprigs of tiny flowers in Ellie's hair. "Looking one's best and feeling assured is a more effective shield than most realize. It will serve you well tonight."

Another variation on Artemis's rules for being bold: dressing to feel confident was a form of wielding one's shield.

"I will look a mess day in and day out when I have to return to Shropshire."

A little softness entered Rose's eyes. "I'll teach you all I can before you go."

"Thank you." Ellie stood and took a reassuring breath. "I could not have done anything I have this last week without you."

Rose motioned her out. "The surest way to lose a battle is to arrive late."

Ellie crossed paths with Artemis in the corridor.

"I debated with Rose about the wisdom of putting you in that particular shade of green." She gave her a quick look over. "Rose was absolutely correct. You look stunning."

"I do like Rose. She can be reticent, but as I've come to know her a little, I have come to realize she is remarkably kind, and she is, as she declared that first day, exceptionally good at what she does."

"Yes, she is."

"How did you come to know her?" Ellie asked.

They walked together down the corridor toward the stairs. "Her uncle is valet to . . . well, actually, to Charlie's oldest brother." Artemis hooked her arm through Ellie's as they walked down the stairs. "I was in need of a lady's maid who shared more of the vision I had for myself. And Wilson, her uncle, is rather famous, which seems like an odd thing for gentleman's personal servant, but he is a legend. I asked, through Lady Lampton, if her husband's valet might be bothered to offer a recommendation. He told me I could do no better than his niece Rose. He was absolutely correct. She has no equal."

Ellie ventured to say what she absolutely would not have dared to a month earlier. "For someone you swear you adamantly dislike, you are connected to Charlie Jonquil in seemingly countless ways."

"Do not remind me. It seems I can't escape that man."

They had reached the front entryway, where Artemis's brother was waiting, his wife at his side. "Am I the one you're so upset you can't escape? If you would prefer, I could send you back to Falstone Castle, then it would be our brother-in-law you could not escape."

Artemis quite dramatically made a show of being horrified at the possibility. Mr. Lancaster laughed. Mrs. Lancaster smiled at their antics.

The tone amongst them remained light and teasing all the way to the Beauford Square. Ellie hadn't the first idea how they were meant to find the Hugheses in the large theater, but her companions did not seem to be suffering under the weight of the same ignorance. They moved through the crowd of theatergoers without hesitation or uncertainty and were soon in the company of the very people they were looking for.

Their welcome was that of dear friends reunited. Even Ellie, who had met the Hugheses only briefly at a ball, was received with warmth.

Newton always looked handsome, but he was dressed particularly well this evening, and his smile was warm and personal. The seven of them stood in a friendly, intimate clump.

After a moment, Mrs. Carter passed and offered her greetings to Mrs. Hughes.

Mr. Hughes spoke first. "Mrs. Carter, are you acquainted with the Lancasters and Miss Ellie Napper?"

Mrs. Carter nodded slowly, her gaze narrowing with curiosity. "We hail from near the same village. I heard you had become acquainted with Miss Ellie."

The Hugheses exchanged looks of confusion before returning their gaze to Mrs. Carter.

"She is a friend of the family," Mrs. Hughes said. "Why do you assume our acquaintance is of short duration?"

Oh, they were adept at this dance. With that simple question, Mrs. Hughes had undermined the rumor and put one who had been embracing it on the defensive. And she had managed it without being rude or unkind.

"Forgive me," Mrs. Carter said. "I had not realized the connection was of long standing." She turned and looked at Ellie. "A pleasure to see you again."

Ellie dipped a curtsy. "And I you."

The same thing repeated a few times. Sometimes the Hugheses took the lead, sometimes the Lancasters. The encounters played out in different ways, but the point was always the same. It would not take long for the whispers in Society to shift. The next day, ladies would be talking over their teacups, not about poor put-upon Newton Hughes being so mercilessly tricked by a presumptuous mushroom, but about how the gullible among Society had actually believed those rumors, conveniently ignoring the fact that most of those doing the whispering had believed the gossip themselves.

The group was still surrounded by friends, acquaintances, and the curious when Lillian had the audacity to thrust her company upon them all.

She looked at Ellie with what could only be described as pity. "Mother and Father were worried you would be here," she said, doing a remarkable job of making herself seem as though she actually cared about her sister. "I promised them I would come see if you were in attendance and attempt to extract you from this unfortunate plot of yours."

"And what plot would that be?" Artemis asked.

Lillian pressed a hand to her heart. "You cannot be ignorant of Elfrida's plan to ensnare Mr. Hughes. I only wish I had realized it sooner."

"I fear you will have to be more specific." Artemis was not giving an inch.

"I cannot bear the thought of her playing Mr. Hughes such a dirty trick. He's a good, kind, and caring gentleman. He ought not be treated this way."

"Are you suggesting my son is a dunderhead?" Mrs. Hughes asked, her tone both icy and challenging.

"Oh, heavens, no." Lillian didn't pause for even the length of a breath.

"Then what is it you are implying?"

Lillian eyed all the gathering, clearly determining whether or not she had an attentive audience. "Ellie has designs on your son. She has been pushing her company on him, forcing a connection that does not exist."

"Whatever do you mean?" Mrs. Hughes asked. "A connection certainly does exist. Indeed, I have been telling these good people, 'Look how good of a dear friend she has been to our family.'"

They were wielding their shields, but was it working?

Lillian turned to Ellie once more. "Why are you keeping silent while they say these things? You know it is not true. Surely, they know it isn't."

The shields were proving insufficient. The time had come to return fire. "Step carefully, dearest sister. You are tiptoeing terribly close to calling Mrs. Hughes a liar."

For the first time, Lillian showed a little hesitancy. "I am certain she realizes that was not my intent."

Mrs. Hughes stood in firm silence.

Mr. Hughes spoke on her behalf. "I confess, I began to worry myself that you were about to make that precise accusation, Miss Napper."

Lillian's eyes pulled wide, clearly uncertain what to do next.

"I would like to add," Artemis said, "you know I am privy to a tidbit about your behavior toward Mr. Newton Hughes that I am absolutely certain you wouldn't want to be generally known. Unlike the rumors and whispers you have been instrumental in spreading, my information is entirely true. Proceed with caution, for my reach is far greater than yours." Artemis spoke that last sentence chillingly, with an authority that could not be questioned.

Lillian slipped away, swiftly and without her usual grace. Ellie, though grateful her name was beginning to be cleared, did not for a moment believe she had endured her final reckoning with her sister. When her sojourn in Bath was over, she would return to Shropshire. To her family home.

To her vindictive, angry sister.

CHAPTER SEVENTEEN

NEWTON WAS BEGINNING TO BREATHE more easily. A week had passed since Lillian's rumors had made their debut. A week in which Artemis, her family, Ellie, Newton, and his parents had been hard at work countering the whispers. Artemis had predicted a fortnight would be required to manage their ends. She had overestimated. Ellie was already being warmly received by all of Bath's hostesses. Newton had, himself, heard her referred to as "a friend of the Hugheses."

She was well received, well-liked, and welcomed. Newton's parents had even warmed to her, something he'd not have thought possible a month ago. They would not be overjoyed or even vaguely approving of the idea of a match between himself and Ellie, but he found more and more that *he* would not dislike such a match. Not in the least.

How easily he could imagine himself sitting down with her after a day spent studying the law and telling her what he'd learned. He knew enough of her clever mind to be certain they would never struggle for conversation, even on topics unfamiliar to one or both of them. With the large selection of bookstores in London at her disposal, Ellie would enjoy devouring literature and academic texts. And being in London, she would have the company of Artemis and the Huntresses. She would be able to participate in the Season. She would be away from her family and away from her sister.

Life would change so quickly for her and so entirely. He knew he hadn't any real right to place himself in the future he hoped she dreamed of, but he wanted to believe there was a chance he was part of that already.

They had first met as part of a ruse. From that bit of deception had grown a friendship as real as any he had experienced. And from that friendship had come love. Though it had taken him a while to admit it to himself, he loved her. He could not imagine not having her in his life.

He did not consider himself a coward, but he was struggling to summon courage enough to go to the Lancasters' home to tell her how he felt, tell her of his wishes and dreams. How often those in new or uncertain relationships were lectured for not simply "telling the other person how you feel" or "just talking more." It was easy to offer that kind of advice when someone else's happiness was at risk. Relationships always seemed simple when viewed from the outside.

The door to the book room, where he had been sitting while his thoughts spun in endless circles, opened, and the butler appeared in the doorway. "Your presence has been requested in the drawing room."

Newton dipped his head in acknowledgment. "I will be there directly."

He welcomed the distraction. He'd come to no useful conclusions about how to proceed with his newly identified feelings for Ellie. A change of scenery and company other than his own would do him good.

He made his way to the drawing room, unsure who was calling but not particularly worried. The distraction would be welcome no matter who provided it. Inside, conversing with his parents, was a gentleman he recognized immediately due to a striking family resemblance. This was one of Charlie's brothers. Jason, if he was not mistaken. Jason, the one he had sent a message to in London. The barrister.

"Mr. Jonquil," Newton said, holding out his hand. "A pleasure to see you."

Jason had risen and shook Newton's hand. "And you."

They were quickly situated. Jason, true to character, spoke without awkwardness or pretense. "I was most intrigued by your letter," he said to Newton. "I, of course, am quite partial to the law myself and will always encourage any gentleman of sense, determination, and integrity to pursue that occupation if he is able. Your letter showed you have given the matter great thought, which bodes well. Too many gentlemen take up the law simply because they need a profession and don't care for the dangers of the army or the boredom of the church. I'm always pleased to hear it has been chosen because it is preferred rather than because it is what is left."

Father and Mother were both watching Newton with curiosity.

"You wrote to Mr. Jonquil of your ambitions?" Father asked.

Newton nodded. "I felt he could provide me with the best understanding of what the pursuit involves and the type of gentlemen I'm likely to interact with, as well as what will be expected of me while I pursue that goal."

Mother shook her head the tiniest bit, an affectation she employed when baffled by something. "You have spoken of pursuing the law, but I had not realized you were so determined to do so. I suppose I had always assumed it was more of an idle curiosity."

How could his parents possibly think that? He'd spoken of it for several years, with increasing focus and emphasis over the last six months. Just since being here in Bath, he had discussed the idea with them more and more. Of course, until recently, he had tended to back down from disagreements with his parents. Ellie's bravery had taught him the value of being firm in his own defense. Artemis's tutoring had taught him how.

"I assure you it is anything but an idle curiosity," he said. "I fully intend to pursue this, and I mean to do so in as logical and intelligent a manner as possible. Charlie has always spoken highly of his brother Jason, and no member of his family has ever seemed the least ashamed of having a barrister among them."

Jason, who had been watching this exchange with the focus and intrigue of a man with a natural inclination toward analysis, reentered the conversation. "Your son did express in his letter your concerns with this profession. I can tell he does not wish to bring any sort of dishonor on your family, nor does he want to cause you pain. His thoughtfulness impressed me. Many gentlemen from remarkable families populate my profession. It is not looked down on. It does not prevent any of us from receiving social invitations or from being part of Society. When my children are of age, they will not be prevented from making their bows. If Newton chooses to pursue this, you will suffer no disgrace. Assuming, of course, he conducts himself in matters of the law with integrity and honesty."

Mother ruffled up a bit. "Of course he would. Our Newton has an unwavering sense of integrity."

Jason sat in calm stillness, but Newton had known Charlie too long to not recognize the twinkle in those Jonquil eyes. The brothers were different from each other in many ways, but they were so alike in so many others. Jason had known that casting the tiniest bit of a cloud over the question of Newton's moral fitness for pursuing this profession would bring his parents to his defense faster than trying to drag them there with arguments in favor of the profession.

Jason turned his attention to Newton. "Do you know which Inn of Court you wish to attach yourself to for your studies?"

Newton kept his expression as neutral as Jason did, participating in the discussion as if it were academic and not fraught with pitfalls. Jason himself, after all, was attached to an Inn of Court professionally as a working barrister. To name any one other than his would be something of an insult. Fortunately for Newton,

Jason belonged to Lincoln's Inn, which was the one he most wished to be connected to. "My highest aspirations are for Lincoln's, of course. But I do not know if I'll be so fortunate as to find someone who will speak for me when I apply there."

"I am not my oldest brother," Jason said. "You needn't undertake a verbal sparring match to gain my approval or keep my interest. Lincoln's Inn is a fine place to begin your education. And I would be happy to stand as your champion there."

Newton maintained his composure, limiting himself to words of gratitude. He could tell by his parents' expressions that they did not fully understand the enormity of what had just occurred. He had, with a single letter and a single conversation, secured himself the recommendation he needed to begin his studies, something many gentlemen struggled to obtain. It was the first of several steps placing him on the path toward the future he wished for.

Jason continued with as much directness as ever. "The matter of your education will take two or three years, depending on how quickly you take in the information you need and how much time you spend in this pursuit. During those years, you will not be able to undertake any other sort of profession in order to obtain funds to live on. I do not imagine that will be an issue, considering your family's financial stability. However, I feel it prudent to at least mention that particular difficulty in case there are extenuating circumstance of which I am unaware."

This time, it was Father who spoke in his defense. "Our estate is quite profitable, and all of my children are provided for generously from that estate. Newton would have ample to live on without any profession, including the law. He could most certainly support himself while studying whatever he wished."

Again, Jason dipped his head and maintained a neutral expression anyone truly acquainted with his family would be able to easily see through. "While I realize your family has a residence in Town, it has been judged best by a majority of those studying at the Inns of Court to reside in close proximity to their selected Inn. Many newly arrived gentlemen obtain lodging together, allowing for comradery between them and opportunities for discussing what they have learned and studied. For some, it is also a means of stretching their lean incomes. You will not need a vast deal of room, as you will not have time for entertaining callers. You will spend countless long nights reviewing topics you have learned about in lecture and whilst listening to discussions amongst the professionals at the Inn of Court."

"I understand," Newton said.

"And while the vast majority of those undertaking a legal education are single gentlemen in no hurry to find themselves attached or married, it does happen on occasion that a gentleman's romantic pursuits overlap with his professional ones. That, I will warn you, would complicate things. You will not have a great deal of time, and any young lady you wish to court would likely feel neglected by that."

Mother waved that off. "He does not have an understanding with anyone. He is quite unattached."

Jason eyed Newton a little sidelong. He did not, however, say more on that matter. What had Charlie said to him? What did Charlie think he knew? Newton had only recently acknowledged to himself a preference for Ellie's company. At the time Charlie left, Newton had not truly understood the depths of those feelings himself.

Newton thought it best to change the topic. "We mean to remain here in Bath another fortnight. If I hie myself directly to London afterward, would that timing allow me to begin my studies forthwith?"

Jason nodded. "Simply call on me at my office. I will see to it you can begin immediately."

"I cannot thank you enough. This is something I've dreamed of but did not know how to make happen."

Jason smiled, something Charlie insisted he didn't use to do often. "I had help and encouragement when I began my pursuit. I'm happy to do the same for someone else."

They all remained and chatted amicably for a little bit longer before Jason declared that he needed to be on his way, as he was expected back in London in a couple of days' time. He had, then, made the trip from Town specifically for this discussion. He might just as easily have sent a letter. That, Newton had no doubt, was Charlie's doing.

After their guest left, Mother and Father wasted no time speaking of the visit. They declared it remarkable that Jason had made the trip specifically for a visit to this house. They discussed in tones far more approving than they had before Newton's wish to study the law. He did not doubt they were still not entirely enthusiastic about the idea of one of their children in a professional pursuit, but they had warmed to the idea enough that he could, with confidence in their support, pursue it.

He wished he could speak to them of his thoughts about Ellie, but he could not clear his thoughts of Jason's words of warning.

He wanted to build a future with Ellie, but perhaps he'd best not do so until he could give her all of himself, not merely what he could manage outside of his studies. She deserved to be courted and loved, to have the full attention and time of the gentleman of her choosing. He would not be able to avoid a degree of neglect. He could not bear the thought of causing her pain by spending two or three years in such a state of distraction.

He knew the life he wanted. But he wasn't entirely sure how to claim it.

CHAPTER EIGHTEEN

NEWTON'S FEET CARRIED HIM TO the Lancasters' house but not to call on any member of that family. He wanted to see Ellie. He needed to. She would be happy for the offer Jason Jonquil had made that morning, and she would understand how much it meant to him.

She was the first to arrive in the drawing room. The door was left open, but they still had a great deal of privacy. This was the time to speak of more personal things, before they had an audience.

"Charlie's brother called on my parents and me," he said without preamble.

"I didn't realize he had a brother in Bath."

Newton wasn't being clear or eloquent. "Jason, the brother who called, wasn't in Bath but in London. He is a barrister, and he and his family live in Town most of the year."

"He traveled all the way from London?" Ellie looked appropriately impressed. She sat and motioned for him to do the same. "That is not a journey made in a single day."

"I was as surprised as you are," he said. "Charlie delivered to him a letter I wrote asking questions about his Inn of Court and the logistics of studying to be a barrister. I had hoped for a response of some kind. Imagine my surprise when that response proved to be his arrival here."

"It seems Charlie is not the only Jonquil with a caring heart."

Newton nodded. "They are good guns, every last one of them."

"Was Mr. Jason Jonquil's visit an encouraging one?"

The amazement he'd felt during that call swelled once more. "More than encouraging; it was nearly miraculous. He made an airtight case to my parents and has secured, if not their enthusiasm, at least their acceptance. He further offered to recommend me at Lincoln's Inn."

Though Ellie watched him with interest, her confusion was clear. Few understood how one's education in the law was undertaken. He explained, at first intending to keep the details few, but her interest did not wane, neither did her eyes gloss over as so many did when topics uninteresting to them were introduced.

"Mr. Jonquil's offer will save you time and difficulty," Ellie said when he'd finished explaining.

"Quite a bit."

She scooted a little closer, near enough for him to take her hand. "How soon will you begin your law education?"

"I am for London in a fortnight. I will secure lodgings somewhere—Mr. Jonquil indicated several boarding establishments can be found nearby that cater to students of the law. Generally, they place several students in a flat, but it is, apparently, not a miserable arrangement."

"I am so happy for you, Newton."

He studied her expression. "You do not seem entirely happy."

"I *am* happy for you. But I am not particularly overjoyed for me." She stood and paced away, twisting her hands around one another. "My family is returning to Shropshire in two days' time. I have no choice but to go with them. *That* will be, to borrow your phrase, a miserable arrangement."

Newton had known she would eventually have to leave Bath and do so with the people who treated her with such unkindness, but he'd repeatedly pushed that from his thoughts. He ought not to have. He ought to have been thinking of a way to help her. But what could he do? Her father was granted by the law full control over every aspect of her life. She was at his mercy. Newton could do nothing to help her.

He moved to where she stood. "Will you come to London for the Season? You have spoken of wishing to do so."

"Even if my family could afford to do so or had once been willing, I am certain they will not do so now," she said. "I have every reason to believe they blame me for Lillian's fall from grace. Life at home is going to be awful. I know it will be."

He took her hand and raised it to his lips, kissing her knuckles. "I am so sorry, Ellie. I truly am."

She took a slightly shaky breath. "I am not looking forward to the next . . . well, the next *forever*."

Newton took a quick look toward the doorway, making certain it was empty. Finding them momentarily alone, he closed the small distance between the two of them. As she'd done once before in this very room, Ellie leaned against him, resting her head on his shoulder. He set his arms around her. She was soft and warm in his embrace, peaceful. With her, he found the elusive feeling of home.

Standing with her in his arms, he found himself questioning everything. His family provided him with income that would support a family in some degree of comfort. If he abandoned his dreams of being a barrister, he and Ellie could, perhaps, be together. Could he find happiness enough in their connection to push away the disappointment of losing that dream, the tedium of having no occupation? But if he followed *that* dream, would he ever stop regretting losing the dream of *her*?

Ellie was happy for Newton, but her heart was heavy. He'd held her tenderly, expressed a wish to see her in London, but he'd offered no reassurance of his love or his wish for a future together. He intended to find a flat with a group of other students, hardly the lodgings one searched out when wishing to marry.

She wanted to believe she hadn't imagined his feelings growing genuinely more tender toward her. Perhaps, eventually, those feelings would have grown strong enough for him to make anything resembling a promise. But they'd run out of time.

Artemis came upon her as she sat worn down and burdened on the bed in the guest chamber. "You do not seem quite your usual self."

"My family is returning to Shropshire," she said. "My sister's sojourn in Bath has taken a turn for the worse."

Artemis sat beside her. "Imagine that."

Ellie pushed out a breath. "I am absolutely certain they blame me."

"Why admit they caused their own trouble when they can secure a convenient scapegoat?" Artemis shook her head in obvious annoyance. "Your family are not precisely scholars, are they?"

She smiled a little but found her heart wasn't entirely in it. "My life is about to be extremely miserable."

"Not necessarily." Artemis turned a little, facing her more directly. "What if, instead of going to Shropshire to be tortured and mistreated, you came to Northumberland with me and wandered the dusty and drafty corridors of a five-hundred-year-old castle?"

Ellie was too surprised to do anything but narrow her gaze and draw her brows in silence.

"None of my siblings is planning to visit this winter. My sister and brother-in-law, the ones who live there, have their own family to occupy their time and attention. All of the Huntresses have their own homes in which to pass the cold, dark months." Though Artemis was being a bit jestful in her tone and explanation, there was real sadness in her eyes. "It is terribly lonely, Ellie. I've come to actually dread being at the castle."

"And you wish me to join you there?"

She smiled a little uncertainly. "I would be unspeakably grateful."

Ellie didn't dare let herself believe it possible. "Your brother-in-law is known to despise company."

"He won't object," Artemis said.

"You can't be certain of that."

"Actually, I can." Some of her friend's confidence was returning. "I wrote to the duke and duchess asking for their honest feelings on the possibility of my bringing a friend to spend the winter there."

"And what did they say?" Ellie was both eager for and dreading the answer.

"My sister thought it a brilliant idea. She remembers you well from our years in Shropshire and her visits back there since."

The duchess's welcome was not unexpected. "And your brother-in-law?"

"He said, and I quote, 'If having a friend will keep you out of mischief, invite every friend you have.'"

That sounded just grumpy enough to be the Dangerous Duke's verbatim instructions. "He is a little frightening," Ellie admitted.

"Not when you know him better. He can actually be remarkably kind. You'll see."

She doubted it but found herself less worried. "And they would let me stay for the entire winter?"

Artemis nodded, excitement growing in her expression. "And then you can come to London with us for the Season."

"Truly?" She could hardly believe the extent of this offer.

"And I've spoken with Rose, and she is ecstatic at the prospect of spending the next months creating an entire new wardrobe for you to wear in Town. We mean to obtain some fabric and trimming while we're here, as well as materials for a few bonnets. We will be kept quite wonderfully busy."

Her heart fluttered despite her attempts to quiet it. "I cannot possibly impose so much."

"No imposition. I would be indebted to you." Beyond sincere, Artemis sounded almost desperate. Artemis Lancaster, who never seemed anything other than fully and completely self-assured, was nearly pleading for a companion, for a friend. "Please, say you'll come."

"It would be far preferable to Shropshire."

Artemis's eyes lit with hope. "And going to London in the spring won't be miserable either."

"I have always wanted to go to Town."

With mischief in her tone and far too much innocence in her expression, Artemis said, "And Mr. Newton Hughes will be there, quite the fine and fancy student of the law. That must be some motivation."

Hope and hesitation warred in her heart. "I will enjoy seeing him again."

Artemis repeated Ellie's words in an overly prim and proper voice. "'I will enjoy seeing him again.'" She folded her arms across her chest. "Do not attempt to hoodwink me, Ellie. I know you've lost your heart to him."

"His, however, seems quite whole and entirely in his possession."

Artemis eyed her more closely. "Why do you say that?"

"He visited and told me of the progress he'd made in convincing his parents to accept his pursuit of the law, and he spoke with great enthusiasm about securing a flat with other students and beginning his studies." Disappointment washed over her. "He dedicated not a syllable to his hopes for *our* future. I had so hoped he would at least express regret that we'd not had the chance for a true courtship."

"No matter how it began," Artemis said, "your courtship was as genuine as any I've seen. You spent time together, formulated plans together, came to know each other. He might not have spoken of courtship because he feels you've already had one."

Ellie shook her head. "If that were the case, he would have left me with some hope, some semblance of a promise."

"Perhaps he is as unsure of your feelings as you seem to be of his. A bit of bravery would do the both of you a world of good."

Though there was wisdom in her advice, there was also tremendous risk. "Bravery does not guarantee a good outcome."

Artemis offered an empathetic smile. "Cowardice almost always guarantees a poor one."

Ellie knew her friend was correct. Yet, the prospect was frightening. "If I find my bravery and that ends badly, do you have a corner at Falstone Castle where I can cry, curse the fates, and engage in whatever overly dramatic response I find necessary?"

"I regularly indulge in all of those things," Artemis said. "I can show you all the best places to undertake them."

Ellie took a deep breath and resolved herself on two matters: she would accept Artemis's invitation, and before they left Bath, she would find the courage to discover if the feelings of Newton's heart matched her own.

CHAPTER NINETEEN

Mrs. Lancaster was not feeling particularly well that evening, so they all opted to remain at home rather than toss themselves out into the social whirl. Ellie's family would be attending a few smaller events, the last they would be part of before returning to Shropshire. Perhaps she ought to have been a little sad at missing this final opportunity to see them.

She wasn't.

"Entirely understandable," Mr. Lancaster said, having poked his head into the sitting room. "They have caused you no end of trouble. Perhaps, in time, you will wish to see them again, but the fact that they are family does not obligate you to inflict further misery on yourself."

Artemis nodded her wholehearted agreement, having already told Ellie much the same thing.

"And do *you* agree with your sister that I will not be intruding if I join her at Falstone Castle?" Ellie had worried over that.

Mr. Lancaster offered a broad smile, one nearly identical to his youngest sister's. "Adam will grump and grumble a great deal, but pay him no heed. He will be grateful that Artemis has a friend with her."

"Because I am meant to keep her out of mischief?" Ellie asked. "That is what his letter said."

"Despite both of their efforts to appear otherwise, Adam and Artemis are rather fond of each other."

"What a great deal of fiddle-faddle," Artemis said. "Mark my words, ours is a mutual dislike that will one day be legendary."

Mr. Lancaster shook his head. "Good evening, both of you."

"Good evening?" Artemis clicked her tongue and shook her head. "You are retiring so early that I begin to wonder if you aren't secretly ninety years old."

"You age a person, Artemis." He pressed his hand dramatically to his heart. "You age a person."

Artemis laughed and waved him away.

"Your brother dotes on you," Ellie said. "I've often wondered, If I'd had a brother, would he have been so fond of me?"

"I should hope so." Artemis took up her book of fashion plates once more. "Any brother who did not adore you would not be a brother worth having."

Artemis was good for Ellie's too-oft wounded pride. Her own family had dealt it so many felling blows.

"If Rose didn't find my company too tedious when not permitted ample time apart, I would beg her to go over these prints with me and begin planning your new wardrobe."

"I don't think she finds you tedious," Ellie said with a laugh.

Artemis grinned. "Rose says I am best taken in small doses. I cannot entirely disagree with her."

Ellie looked forward to coming to know this remarkable woman better over the winter. She had known so few people. Her circle of acquaintances was expanding in remarkable ways.

A knock sounded at the door. Ellie and Artemis glanced at each other, confused. It was not so late that a caller was improper, but it was a bit odd.

Ellie rose and pulled back the curtain in the tall front-facing window. She saw no carriage, no horse, nothing to indicate who stood at the door, which was not visible from her vantage point. "I suspect we may soon be asked if we are at-home to a ghost."

"Excellent," Artemis said. "I have spent years attempting to find a ghost in my brother-in-law's castle. Nary a one." She clicked her tongue. "A terrible disappointment."

In the next moment, a very confused and extremely intrigued Henson popped his head in the room. "A visitor for Miss Ellie." He shrugged. "He said it weren't improper if Miss Lancaster kept to the room."

"*He?*" Artemis looked to Ellie with wide eyes.

"Who is it?" Ellie asked the butler.

"Mr. Hughes."

She swallowed. "Father or son?"

"Oh." Henson assumed a more proper posture. "Mr. *Newton* Hughes."

"Son," Artemis said, a bit of cheek beneath her unneeded clarification.

Ellie hadn't the first idea what the appropriate thing to do was. Newton felt it acceptable for him to step into the room, but was it truly? She wanted him to stay but didn't wish to undo the work they'd done to uphold her reputation.

"Show him in," Artemis said. "We will all three remain in this room."

Ellie stood rooted to the spot, hardly breathing. What had brought Newton back so soon? When he'd left that afternoon, she'd thought he'd meant to make for London at his earliest opportunity.

He stepped inside. Newton's gaze settled immediately on her. There was something urgent in his expression. Almost panicked.

"What has happened?" she asked. "You were in such good spirits when last I saw you."

"I was a fool when last I saw you." He stopped directly in front of her. "A fool and a coward."

Ellie had felt rather like a coward herself, something she'd hoped to rectify.

"Artemis," Newton tossed over his shoulder, "take pity on me and occupy your attention elsewhere, will you?"

"Not a chance of it," Artemis said. "This is the most excitement we've had in this house all evening."

With a sigh of resignation, he turned back to Ellie.

She smiled empathetically. "Artemis certainly likes to tease, doesn't she?" Choosing to be brave, as she'd told her friend she would be, Ellie reached out and brushed a hand gently along Newton's stubbled cheek. "What has upset you, Newton?"

He set his hand on hers, weaving their fingers, then moved their entwined hands to his lips and brushed the softest of kisses there. "I've been a fool."

"You said that already," Artemis tossed out.

"Stop it," Ellie warned with a laugh.

Apparently, having satisfied her need for mischief, Artemis turned her back to them and took up her fashion plates.

"What makes you think you've been a fool?" Ellie asked quietly.

"I told you of my future plans, as they pertain to my profession, my lodging, my parents' acceptance of it all. But I stopped short of saying what I most wanted to say, most *needed* to say."

She forced a breath in and out. "And what was that?"

Newton closed the small gap between them and slowly set his free arm around her. "I love you, Ellie. I can't tell you when it started or how it began. We were pretending and putting on a show, and somehow, in the midst of it all, the feelings became real and genuine."

"Oh, Newton," she whispered.

"I wanted to tell you all of this, but I know perfectly well what my next years will hold. Jason Jonquil was quite clear about it: long days, an overwhelming workload, little time for friends and family, let alone courtship and love."

She held her breath. How afraid she'd been that he would not return her regard, when all the while, he already did.

"I told myself," he continued, "that I would do best not to say anything. Should you, somehow, not give your heart elsewhere before I was able to at last be the suitor you deserved, I promised myself I would then make my suit in earnest. But, my darling Ellie, I cannot bear the thought of you going to Shropshire without telling you how I feel. My heart would simply wither and die while we were apart."

Ellie held ever tighter to his hand, overwhelmed at the sincerity she saw in his face.

"I expect no return of my regard, and I most certainly don't expect you to set yourself on a shelf to wait for me, but I—"

She set her other hand against his heart. "I'm not going to Shropshire."

Her answer clearly caught him unawares. He didn't have a ready response.

"Artemis has invited me to join her at Falstone Castle until the spring comes. Then we are both going to London for the Season."

"You are?" Hope flooded his voice.

"And I want nothing more during that Season than to see you, as often as you are able."

"That will be shockingly seldom," he warned. "I am told my days will be spent from morning to night at Lincoln's Inn. My only time away will be those few hours at night when I am home. There may be a few soirees or balls now and then but very few."

"I'll be at all of them you are," she said. "I will make certain of it."

"It will never feel like enough," he said.

She leaned against him. His embrace tightened, and he rested his cheek against the top of her head. Ellie closed her eyes, letting the warmth of him wash over her. He'd held her before, and it had felt just the same: utterly perfect.

"I suppose you could always make questionable late-evening calls like this at the house where I'll be staying," Ellie said. "Then I would see you more often."

"If only that house were—" He stopped quite abruptly but didn't release her.

"If only that house were *what?*" she asked.

She felt him take a deep, chest-raising breath. "It is too bold, Ellie. I'll not make so ill-advised a leap as that."

"A wise person once told me that cowardice is all but guaranteed to cost a person what he truly wants." Ellie pulled back the tiniest bit and looked up at him. "I believe we would both do best to be brave."

He slipped free the hand she held and wrapped that arm around her as well. "What if that house were *our* house? What if, instead of trying to find you for an hour during my brief time away from my studies, you were *there*? What if we were together every moment we were able to be?"

She raised an eyebrow. "Are you asking me to share a flat with your fellow law students?"

"No," he said quickly and firmly.

She was teasing him, of course, but she also knew better than to leave so crucial a question unspecified. "You had best tell me quite plainly what it is you *are* asking me."

Newton stepped back and took her hands in his. "Ellie Napper, I am asking you if you'll write to me while you're in Northumberland, and if you'll allow me to write to you." Such an arrangement constituted an understanding between a gentleman and a lady. They both knew as much. "And I'm asking if, when you arrive in London, should you find that your heart wishes to build a life with mine, you will begin that life with me."

She raised up on her toes and kissed his cheek. "I would love nothing more."

He bent his neck swiftly enough to capture her lips before she pulled away. He kissed her gently, tenderly. "When you come to London," he said. "Once you've had time to make certain this is what you want."

"And *you* have had time to do the same." Months of correspondence free of her family's interference and the confusion of a one-time feigned courtship would do their connection good, would strengthen it.

"In London," he said. "I will be counting down the days."

"You could always come visit her here every day for the next two weeks." Artemis spoke, startling them both. "We don't leave for Northumberland until then."

Newton smiled at Ellie. "I would like that."

"So would I," she said.

Newton called at the Lancaster home every day for the next fortnight, delaying his own departure from Bath until after hers. Visiting with her had made the past two weeks an utter joy. She was precisely the person he'd believed her to be based on the glimpses he'd seen of her when not assuming her previous part.

They shared an interest in learning anything and everything. Though Ellie did not object to the possibility of someday traveling, she lit up most when they'd spoken of the hope of family and home and stability. When he spoke of the law, she showed genuine interest and asked insightful questions. When she spoke of her interest in poetry, he found himself delighted to know they had that interest in common. She expressed, with obvious uncertainty at his reaction, a wish to someday write poetry of her own. He told her without hesitation that he truly hoped she wrote mountains of it.

They were more than well suited; they were perfectly matched. He loved her more every time they were together.

The day arrived when Ellie, along with the Lancasters, was to leave Bath. Though Newton's heart ached at knowing they would be separated for a time, he was far from despondent. He felt in his heart of hearts that when she arrived in London, they would never need to be apart again.

The carriage outside was laden with traveling trunks and awaited the Lancaster passengers. Ellie and Newton had slipped into the drawing room, its furniture draped in cloth. He held her in his arms, cherishing these last moments together before their temporary separation.

"I mean to find a flat somewhere near the Inns of Court but in a respectable area," Newton said. "Not one for a bachelor but one you needn't feel the least displeased with."

"You must be terribly confident that I will still wish to marry you in a few months' time." Her tone was too teasing to cause him even the tiniest worry.

"Charlie's brother is a vicar," Newton said. "I mean to have him pray over it."

She laughed. "How many brothers does he have?"

"According to him, hundreds."

Ellie leaned a little more heavily against him. "I'll miss you over the winter. Please don't neglect your promise to write to me."

"I will write you so often you will grow weary of my handwriting."

She pressed a kiss to his jaw, then leaned her forehead against his cheek. "I do love you, you know."

"I know. And I am amazed."

"You shouldn't be. I have excellent taste."

Oh, he adored her. "We are going to be the happiest couple in all of England."

"I know," she said. "And I am amazed."

This was their last private moment until they were together again in London. He brushed his lips lightly over her cheek, wishing he could slow the march of time and remain as they were.

"I miss you already," he whispered.

"But only for a time," she answered as softly and quietly as he.

Newton pressed an almost fragile kiss to her lips. She touched his face lightly, returning his affectionate offering. It was reassurance and encouragement and support all contained in a simple, heart-stopping touch.

He had begun his time in Bath unsure of where his life would take him, browbeaten by his parents, and attempting to avoid miserable entanglements. Fate, in all her magic, had given him a future he had only dreamed of, that his parents approved of, and that he had chosen on his own. He had a future. Soon he would have a home and a wife he loved. He would have Ellie in his life for the rest of his life. A truly magical beginning to a remarkably happy ever after.

ABOUT THE AUTHOR

SARAH M. EDEN IS A *USA Today* best-selling author of witty and charming historical romances, including 2019's *Foreword Reviews* INDIE Awards Gold winner for romance, *The Lady and the Highwayman*, and 2020 Holt Medallion finalist, *Healing Hearts*. She is a two-time Best of State Gold Medal winner for fiction and a three-time Whitney Award winner. Combining her obsession with history and her affinity for tender love stories, Sarah loves crafting deep characters and heartfelt romances set against rich historical backdrops. She holds a bachelor's degree in research and happily spends hours perusing the reference shelves of her local library.